A NEW LOVE

(INN BY THE SEA—BOOK 1)

FIONA GRACE

Fiona Grace

Fiona Grace is author of the LACEY DOYLE COZY MYSTERY series, comprising nine books; of the TUSCAN VINEYARD COZY MYSTERY series, comprising seven books; of the DUBIOUS WITCH COZY MYSTERY series, comprising three books; of the BEACHFRONT BAKERY COZY MYSTERY series, comprising six books; of the CATS AND DOGS COZY MYSTERY series, comprising nine books; of the ELIZA MONTAGU COZY MYSTERY series, comprising nine books (and counting); of the ENDLESS HARBOR ROMANTIC COMEDY series, comprising nine books (and counting); of the INN AT DUNE ISLAND ROMANTIC COMEDY series, comprising five books (and counting); of the INN BY THE SEA ROMANTIC COMEDY series, comprising five books (and counting); and of the MAID AND THE MANSION COZY MYSTERY series, comprising five books (and counting).

Fiona would love to hear from you, so please visit www.fionagraceauthor.com to receive free ebooks, hear the latest news, and stay in touch.

BOOKS BY FIONA GRACE

THE MAID AND THE MANSION COZY MYSTERY
A MYSTERIOUS MURDER (Book #1)
A SCANDALOUS DEATH (Book #2)
A MISSING GUEST (Book #3)
AN UNSOLVABLE CRIME (Book #4)
AN IMPOSSIBLE HEIST (Book #5)

INN BY THE SEA ROMANTIC COMEDY
A NEW LOVE (Book #1)
A NEW CHANCE (Book #2)
A NEW HOME (Book #3)
A NEW LIFE (Book #4)
A NEW ME (Book #5)

THE INN AT DUNE ISLAND ROMANTIC COMEDY
A CHANCE LOVE (Book #1)
A CHANCE FALL (Book #2)
A CHANCE ROMANCE (Book #3)
A CHANCE CHRISTMAS (Book #4)
A CHANCE ENGAGEMENT (Book #5)

ENDLESS HARBOR ROMANTIC COMEDY
ALWAYS, WITH YOU (Book #1)
ALWAYS, FOREVER (Book #2)
ALWAYS, PLUS ONE (Book #3)
ALWAYS, TOGETHER (Book #4)
ALWAYS, LIKE THIS (Book #5)
ALWAYS, FATED (Book #6)
ALWAYS, FOR LOVE (Book #7)
ALWAYS, JUST US (Book #8)
ALWAYS, IN LOVE (Book #9)

ELIZA MONTAGU COZY MYSTERY
MURDER AT THE HEDGEROW (Book #1)
A DALLOP OF DEATH (Book #2)

CHAPTER ONE

Charlotte Moore was *desperate* to sell her house. It just *had to* happen today.

Well, maybe not her *actual* house, but the oil portrait that she had lovingly painted of the art-deco building itself—the oil-on-canvas piece was what she *hoped* would go home with a lucky buyer on this fine spring morning.

The bustling Central Market swap meet in the heart of New York City brimmed with energy. Vendors called out to passersby, their voices mingling with the sounds of laughter and conversation that filled the atmosphere from the crowded sidewalks. The intoxicating scent of street food wafted through the air, drawing crowds to the various food stands. Amid the colorful chaos, customers perused the eclectic assortment of wares on display — antiques, handmade crafts, vintage clothing, and more.

Charlotte was busy setting up her booth. Her long brown hair was pulled back into a loose ponytail, wisps of hair framing her face as she concentrated on arranging her items. Each piece was a window into her soul, and she'd come a long way from finger-painting in Mrs. Gerald's first-grade classroom all those years ago in Brooklyn. Her college years in art school had honed her natural passion, and she hoped that *someone* today would see that shining through. She carefully placed each canvas on an easel or leaned it against the booth's tarp-like walls, ensuring the paintings had enough space to breathe and catch the eyes of potential buyers.

As Charlotte stepped back to survey her work, she felt both pride and anticipation. This was her chance to share her creations with the world and make a name for herself in the competitive art scene.

Do you really want to spend all day in the park, trying to hawk paintings on the street?

Daniel's negative tone still rang in her ears from this morning. Charlotte wished she could shake the echo of her husband's haughty voice. It wasn't as if he were doing anything new and exciting since Amelia had moved out.

"Your pieces are absolutely stunning," a woman commented as she stopped at Charlotte's booth, her eyes wide with admiration.

"Thank you," Charlotte replied warmly, turning, her heart swelling with gratitude. "I'm so glad you like them."

She watched as the woman moved from one painting to another, lingering on a particular piece that featured a serene city landscape bathed in the soft light of twilight. Moments like these that made all the late nights in her studio, the self-doubt, and the sacrifices worth it — knowing that her art could touch someone and bring them a moment of joy or contemplation.

"Would you like to know more about this piece?" Charlotte asked gently, not wanting to interrupt the woman's reverie but eager to engage with a potential customer.

"Please," the woman said, turning her curious gaze toward Charlotte. "It's absolutely captivating."

As Charlotte began to share the story behind the painting, she noticed another potential client approaching her booth. The newcomer took in her artwork, fingers tapping on the screen of his cell phone.

"Ah, this one's lovely," the older gentleman remarked, his fingers tracing the edge of a canvas depicting a tranquil lake at sunrise. "What inspired you to paint this?"

"Thank you," Charlotte beamed, her cheeks flushing with pride. "I wanted to capture the feeling of new beginnings. That moment just as the sun rises and illuminates the world."

The man nodded thoughtfully, his eyes still lingering on the painting. "You've captured it beautifully."

"Would you like me to hold this one for you while you continue browsing?" Charlotte offered, her pulse quickening at the possibility of a sale.

"Let me think about it," the man said, patting his pockets as if calculating his budget. "But I'll definitely consider it."

As he moved on, Charlotte turned to find the first woman gone. Disappointment spiked through her, but she tried to remain optimistic. Each kind word or nod of approval fueled her belief in her talent and the potential for her work to find its way into the hearts and homes of others.

As the day went on, Charlotte found herself conversing with customers, answering questions about her artistic process, and sharing anecdotes about the inspirations behind her creations. She passed out dozens of business cards and even had a deli owner from nearby ask if she painted murals. Each conversation left her feeling more invigorated and confident—and Daniel's naysaying from this morning faded to nothing in her mind.

Charlotte could sense the possibility of a sale growing closer. In the early afternoon, she noticed a tall man in his mid-thirties making his way through the crowd. He carried himself with an air of quiet confidence, his dark eyes alight with curiosity as they darted from one piece of art to another.

"Hi, I'm Charlotte," she said as he approached her booth. "Is there anything specific that's caught your eye?"

The man turned his attention to Charlotte and offered a small, polite smile. "Yes, actually, this one right here," he said, gesturing toward the painting depicting her house at dusk, where the sun cast long shadows on the grass and made slightly eerie hollows of the windows and doors.

"Ah, that's one of my favorites," Charlotte admitted, beaming at his interest. "It's my home. The tranquility and mystery of evenings has always been a source of inspiration for me."

"Remarkable," the man murmured, his eyes never leaving the painting. "You've managed to capture the essence of this moment so perfectly."

"Thank you," Charlotte replied, moved by his words. She could sense his genuine appreciation for her work, and it made her heart race with anticipation. What seemed like a simple interaction felt charged with possibility, as if it could be the start of something bigger—maybe a sale!

After a moment, the man pulled out his phone, turned so that the painting was at his back, and snapped a quick photo of himself standing by the painting. "I hope you don't mind me taking a picture, but I wanted to remember this piece. It truly is exceptional."

"Of course not," Charlotte said, flattered. "I'm glad you like it so much. If you were interested in b—"

"Oh, no, no," he said, cutting her off. "But I have a lot of online followers who will love it. I get content, you get free exposure. Win-win."

Charlotte fumbled for a business card. "Oh, um, okay. Well, my social media is here on my card…"

"Thank you for sharing your talent," the man said before suddenly turning on his heel and walking away, disappearing into the bustling swap meet crowd. He hadn't taken her card.

Charlotte blinked, taken aback by his abrupt departure. She had been so sure that this interaction would lead to a sale or a commission, but instead, all she was left with were questions—and a rising sense of annoyance.

Unable to shake off her unease, Charlotte scanned the nearby crowd for the man, considering whether she should follow him and confront him about his intentions. But ultimately, she knew she couldn't abandon her booth and the other people who might be interested in her art. With a deep breath, she decided to let it go, even as her mind continued to wrestle with the implications of his actions. This was definitely not turning out to be her day.

Refocus. Stay positive.

The swap meet seemed to pulse with life, and she tried to recenter herself in the energetic, beating heart of New York City. A breeze rustled through the rows of colorful tents, carrying with it the scent of hot pretzels and fried dough. A street performer had gathered a crowd. Charlotte stood at her booth, letting new anticipation and excitement bubble within her. She still had potential customers browsing her paintings.

"Excuse me," a voice said, pulling Charlotte from her thoughts. She turned to see a woman in her forties admiring one of the paintings. "This is lovely. How much is it?"

"Thank you," Charlotte replied, trying to regain her composure. Then, she realized that there had been a question there—the price! "It's two hundred dollars."

"Such wonderful colors," the woman continued, unaware of the gnawing tension in Charlotte's chest. "You have a real talent."

"Thank you again," Charlotte managed, forcing a smile onto her face. But her mind was elsewhere, still grappling with the selfie and the man's abrupt departure.

"I'll take it."

Charlotte could have leapt for joy. "Oh! Absolutely. Cash or card?"

As she wrapped up the sale for the woman, Charlotte was mired in a mix of excitement and concern. Excitement because someone had shown genuine interest in her art, and concern because of the effort she might have put into this day for such little return.

"Here you go," she said, handing the painting to the woman. "I hope you enjoy it."

"Thank you! This will look perfect in my living room," the woman replied with a smile before walking away.

Well, it was something—one customer.

Charlotte felt her muscles tense as she scanned the crowd, searching for any sign of the man who had left her so unsettled. The cacophony of laughter, bargaining, and rustling bags filled her ears. She plopped down in her folding chair and took a sip of the sweet, tangy lemonade that she'd purchased earlier, its coolness a balm against the burning questions in her mind.

"Charlotte, are you alright?" a familiar voice asked. It was her friend and fellow artist, Sarah, who had a regular booth just four down from Charlotte's own.

"Um, yeah," Charlotte replied hesitantly. "Just... something strange happened."

"Strange how?" Sarah asked, concern etched on her face as she glanced around the bustling swap meet.

"Someone took a photo with one of my paintings, posted it online, and then basically said 'thanks for the content' and left," Charlotte explained, biting her lip.

The petite blonde winced. "Ugh. An influencer. I get those, too. Perhaps they'll come back later?" Sarah suggested, trying to ease her friend's worries.

"Maybe," Charlotte sighed, still unable to shake off her annoyance.

"I gotta run. I have a lunch meeting. Don't you have a meeting of your own today?" Sarah grinned widely, and Charlotte almost regretted telling her friend the secret. Not even Daniel knew it.

Charlotte checked her watch. Her chest tightened. She'd been trying to keep her mind off of *the meeting*, too. But Sarah was right.

"Yep. Four o'clock. With the gallery owners at Ashwood."

"Ooh, good luck, girl!"

With a wave, Sarah was gone, and Charlotte caught sight of a young couple approaching her booth.

"Your work is stunning," the woman from the couple said, admiring one of Charlotte's paintings. "How much is it?"

"Thank you," Charlotte replied, forcing a smile as she tried to focus on the present. "That particular piece is $300."

The woman nodded, turning to her partner for agreement. They exchanged whispers, their heads tilted toward each other, while Charlotte's thoughts flip-flopped between the mysterious photo-taker and her meeting at Ashwood Fine Arts .

"It's beautiful," the woman murmured. "Don't you think so, dear?" She patted the arm of her companion, who smiled indulgently at her.

"Alright, we'll take it," the man declared. He reached for his wallet, ready to seal the deal. As Charlotte carefully wrapped the painting, she found that her new anxiety over the Ashwood meeting eclipsed her excitement over a second sale.

"Thank you so much," Charlotte said to the couple, handing them their newly purchased artwork. They smiled in return, both parties pleased with the transaction.

"Keep up the incredible work," the woman encouraged as they walked away, arm in arm.

"Time will tell," she whispered to herself, watching the crowd ebb and flow around her. As she turned her attention back to her booth, she felt the weight of that unknown future resting heavily on her shoulders. Ashwood had been a hard meeting to book, but she'd managed through persistence—scoring a single chance. If you didn't make a good first impression, Ashwood didn't give you another shot.

As the swap meet began to wind down, Charlotte packed up her booth, checking her watch again to find that she had plenty of time to make her meeting. She'd be early, in fact.

"Focus on what's next," she whispered to herself, securing the last of her paintings in the car. The meeting at the art gallery was an important opportunity, one she couldn't afford to let slip away.

She climbed into the driver's seat, her heart pounding with anticipation for the possibilities ahead. She checked her phone for the first time since the swap meet had begun, and saw that the only notification was a missed call from her daughter, Amelia. Charlotte texted back that she would call her later, and as she revved the engine and pulled away from the swap meet, Charlotte pushed back her uncertainty; the road before her was filled with unexpected twists and turns, but she knew that she had the talent and determination to navigate it all.

"Ashwood," she murmured, "here I come."

CHAPTER TWO

Charlotte took a deep breath as she stood in front of the imposing glass doors of the prestigious Ashwood Art Gallery. The sunlight refracted through the door, casting a prism of colors on the pristine sidewalk and causing her heart to flutter with nervous excitement. She clutched her portfolio tightly against her chest, her palms dampening the leather cover. This was the opportunity she had been waiting for – a chance to showcase her art in one of the city's most renowned galleries.

"Alright, Charlotte," she whispered to herself, "This is your moment." With a determined nod, she pushed open the door and stepped into the gallery.

The interior of Ashwood Art Gallery was a balance of modern elegance and more classic design. High ceilings allowed for an airy ambiance, while the soft glow of recessed lighting bathed the main gallery in a warm, inviting light. The scent of polished hardwood and fresh flowers hung in the air, enveloping the space.

As Charlotte walked further into the room, her eyes were drawn to the vibrant colors of the displayed artwork. A large abstract painting of bold red and blue strokes commanded attention from its central position on one wall, while delicate watercolors of serene landscapes adorned another. Still farther, a grouping of marble pedestals showcased a series of sculptures. The diverse assortment of styles and mediums spoke to the gallery's commitment to celebrating the unique voices of its artists. Charlotte hoped that, after today, she would be among them.

It wasn't just the visual experience of Ashwood that captured Charlotte's senses, but also the subtle sounds echoing throughout the space. The gentle footsteps of the few visitors over the hardwood floors, the hushed whispers, the almost-too-low-to-be-heard classical music, and the faint rustle of a brochure being flipped through all contributed to the gallery's soothing atmosphere. It was a complete 180 from being at the swap meet.

"Welcome to Ashwood Fine Arts," said a sophisticated voice behind her. Charlotte turned to see an impeccably dressed woman, her silver hair pulled back into a sleek bun, offering her a cool smile.

"Thank you," Charlotte said, her voice strained and a little squeaky. She extended her hand to the woman, revealing her portfolio tucked under her arm. "I'm Charlotte Moore. I have an appointment to present my artwork."

"Ah, yes, Mrs. Moore. We've been expecting you," the woman replied, her eyes briefly flicking toward the portfolio. "I'm Lillian Ashwood."

"Oh! You're the owner."

Lillian's smile grew tight. "Yes. Myself and my husband, Aaron. Come with me, please." She led Charlotte further into the gallery, weaving around the main floor.

As they walked, Charlotte couldn't help but feel dwarfed by the grandeur of her surroundings. Was she as good as the artists displayed here? It was a world she had longed to be part of for years, and now, as she clutched her portfolio tighter, she hoped that her own work could find its place among these esteemed creations.

Lillian guided her to a small, private room adorned with minimalist furnishings and pristine white walls. A few other people were waiting inside at a long conference table, their expressions neutral and professional. Charlotte swallowed hard, her pulse quickening as she handed over her portfolio to Lillian. She didn't see Aaron Ashwood at the table—was he? Charlotte should recognize the Ashwoods from their constant appearance in local media, but she hadn't immediately known who Lillian was.

"Please, have a seat." Lillian Ashwood gestured to a vacant chair, and Charlotte obliged. Her fingers gripped the edge of the seat, knuckles turning white as she watched the gallery staff flip through the pages of her portfolio, their expressions betraying little interest in her work.

Each passing second felt like an eternity to Charlotte. The soft hum of the air conditioning battled against the pounding of her heart in her ears. Her eyes darted from one staff member to another, searching for any hint of approval or admiration.

"Your use of color is quite interesting," one of them remarked, his tone lacking enthusiasm. Another offered a nod, but Charlotte couldn't tell if it was out of politeness or genuine appreciation.

As the gallery staff continued to scrutinize her paintings, Charlotte's thoughts raced with questions and doubts. What if they didn't like her work? What if all her efforts had been for naught? She tried to quiet the negative voice in her head, but it persisted, growing louder with each passing moment.

"Mrs. Moore," Lillian finally said, closing the portfolio and placing it on the table before her. Charlotte's heart skipped a beat as she looked up, eyes wide with anticipation.

"While we appreciate the effort you've put into your work and understand its personal significance to you," the silver-haired woman began, her voice devoid of warmth and enthusiasm, "it simply does not fit the artistic direction our gallery is currently pursuing."

Charlotte felt as if she'd been slapped in the face. Her breath hitched, and she struggled to find words. "I... I don't understand," she stammered, her voice barely audible. "I thought Aaron Ashwood would be here, as well. Is he not?"

"Your art is lovely, but we're looking for something more innovative – something that challenges the boundaries of traditional mediums and techniques," the man beside Lillian explained, his tone kinder yet firm. He ignored her question about Aaron, and she could only surmise that *the* Aaron Ashwood saw this meeting as beneath him. "It's just not what we're seeking at the moment."

As the words sunk in, Charlotte's world seemed to crumble around her. She had poured her heart and soul into her paintings, hoping they would resonate with those who viewed them. Yet here she was, being told her work wasn't good enough, that it didn't meet the standards of Ashwood. Nor warrant a meeting with both of the gallery heads. She felt a lump in her throat, threatening to choke her.

Daniel's voice niggled at the back of her mind. She pushed it away.

"Is there anything I can improve? Or perhaps a different series of paintings I could submit?" Charlotte asked, desperation lacing her voice. If only there was a chance, a glimmer of hope that her work could still find a place in this prestigious gallery.

"Unfortunately, Mrs. Moore, we cannot offer any guidance beyond suggesting that you explore different opportunities as an artist," Lillian replied, her eyes void of empathy. "I know many artists of your caliber who find success in the commercial space—window murals, perhaps?"

"Right," Charlotte nodded, her cheeks flushing with embarrassment as she realized they saw her as little more than an amateur. A single tear threatened to escape the corner of her eye, but she blinked it away, refusing to let them see her crumble under the weight of their dismissal. Charlotte swallowed the lump in her throat. She was too shocked to reply to Lillian's slight. With trembling hands, she reached for her portfolio, her vision blurring as unshed tears threatened to spill over.

"Thank you for considering my work," she whispered, clutching the portfolio tightly to her chest as if it were a shield against the crushing weight of rejection.

The gallery staff exchanged glances before Lillian cleared her throat. "We appreciate your effort, Mrs. Moore, but our clientele is looking for something more... cutting-edge," she said dismissively, a bored expression on her face.

"Of course, I understand," Charlotte replied, her voice barely a whisper. She tried to maintain her composure as she stood, but the indifference in their eyes stung like a slap in the face. It seemed that the passion and emotion she poured into her art meant nothing in the cold, calculated world of commercial viability.

"Thank you for your time," the younger staff member said with a patronizing smile, and it was clear they had moved on from Charlotte and her artwork, dismissing her as just another struggling artist not worth their time or consideration.

As she turned to leave the gallery, this time unescorted, each step felt heavier than the last. The vibrant colors of the artwork on display seemed to taunt her, a cruel reminder of the place her own creations would never hold. The once elegant decor now felt suffocating, pressing in on her from all sides as her disappointment morphed into a deep sense of defeat.

In that moment, Charlotte realized that her dreams of success and recognition hinged on the whims of those who valued commerce over passion—a sobering thought. And as she stepped out into the fading afternoon light, the door clicking shut behind her, a single question echoed through her mind: was it worth it?

The warm breeze that tugged at Charlotte's hair as she stepped onto the sidewalk seemed to mirror her own inner turmoil. Her mind swirled with a cacophony of thoughts, each more disheartening than the last. Was her art truly not good enough? Had she been fooling herself all these years, believing in her talent when it ultimately meant nothing to those who guarded the gates?

"Excuse me," a passerby murmured, brushing past her as she stood there, lost in thought. The interruption snapped Charlotte back to the present moment, and she jolted with a sense of embarrassment. Here she was, standing on a busy street, allowing the opinions of strangers to shake her very foundations.

"Get a hold of yourself, Charlotte," she muttered under her breath, willing her racing heart to slow down. As much as she wanted to believe in her art, to know that it had worth beyond the opinions of gallery staff, the sting of rejection sat heavy on her shoulders. The weight of their dismissal threatened to crush her spirit entirely—if she let it.

Head bowed, Charlotte took one last glance at the gallery she had once viewed as the pinnacle of her dreams. With a deep breath, she made the decision to leave it behind and just deal with the crushing disappointment that had come to define her day.

"Thanks for nothing, Ashwood Fine Arts," she murmured. And with that, she turned on her heel and began to walk away, her every step heavy with the burden of rejection. She moved toward her SUV, each step heavier than the last. The vibrant colors of the city seemed to fade around her, leaving a dull grayness that matched her mood. She reached into her pocket and fumbled with her keys, fingers clumsy in her haste to escape the scene of her disappointment.

"Stupid, stupid," she muttered under her breath, berating herself for having believed that her art could make an impact. "Why did I even bother?"

Finally unlocking her car, she slid into the driver's seat. As she gripped the steering wheel, her knuckles turning white, she thought of the gallery staff's feedback.

"Something new and exciting," they had said. But what did that even mean?

"Maybe they're right," Charlotte whispered, the words painfully torn from her throat. "Maybe I'm just not good enough."

Her mind raced as she considered her options. Should she continue pursuing her art despite the seemingly insurmountable obstacles before her? Or should she give up on her dreams entirely, accepting that her talent simply wasn't enough?

Daniel always says I should give up this silly hobby, Charlotte thought. *What's the point of chasing a dream that's out of reach?*

For a moment, her heart ached with the endless possibilities she could've explored if only her art had been accepted. The exhibitions, the potential collectors, the chance to share her work with the world - all of it now seemed like a cruel illusion. Charlotte turned the key in the ignition and the engine roared to life as she fought back tears, the taste of disappointment lingering in the air.

Charlotte pulled away from the curb and glanced at the rearview mirror, watching as the gallery disappeared from sight, taking with it the hopes she'd carried for so long.

CHAPTER THREE

The familiar landmarks that marked Charlotte's journey home blurred by in a wash of greens and browns. She couldn't shake the disappointing outcome of the art gallery meeting from her thoughts; she had poured her heart and soul into those paintings, only to be met with polite disinterest. Add that to the strange man who'd used her art as a photo backdrop, and her day was well and truly spoiled.

Her brow furrowed as she reviewed the conversation at Ashwood over and over again in her head, seeking any clues to where she might have gone wrong. She had always been her own harshest critic, but this was more than just self-doubt. The opinion of the Ashwood staff seemed to mean that there was something fundamentally lacking in her work, and yet Charlotte couldn't quite put her finger on what it was.

Traffic was blessedly light, and the miles flew by. It wasn't long until she was just a few blocks from home, both dreading having to recount her day to Daniel—and hear about how, despite her sales, she'd be better off giving up on painting—and eagerly anticipating a nice, long bath and a glass of wine.

As she pulled into the driveway, she was startled to notice Daniel's car parked askew in the driveway, its trunk thrown open and boxes and luggage piled high within. Her heart stuttered at the sight, confusion washing over her like an unwelcome tide. She blinked rapidly, trying to clear her vision and make sense of what she was seeing.

"Daniel?" she called out hesitantly as she parked beside him and got out of her car. She peered into the open garage.

There was no response, save for the gentle rustling of leaves in the breeze. As Charlotte stood there, her stomach did a flip. This didn't look like a garage cleanout—that was Daniel's own personal luggage. The set he kept in the master bedroom closet for when they traveled.

With a deep breath to steady herself, Charlotte approached the front door, her heart pounding in her chest like a drumbeat. As she pushed the front door open, she was greeted by the sight of even more boxes in the foyer, their stark cardboard edges seeming to mock her from every corner.

"Daniel?" she called again, her voice wavering slightly as she moved further into the house.

"In here," came his reply, soft and laden with both surprise and an unfamiliar heaviness.

Charlotte followed the sound of his voice to the living room, where Daniel stood amid a sea of belongings, his eyes downcast and shoulders slumped. His tall frame seemed smaller somehow, as though weighed down by the gravity of the situation that surrounded them.

"Daniel, what's going on?" Charlotte asked, her confusion rapidly growing as she tried to make sense of the scene before her.

He hesitated for a moment, running a hand through his hair before looking up to meet her gaze. "I wanted to avoid this," he said, sighing. "I think... I think we need to talk, Charlotte."

"About what?" Her voice cracked as she spoke, the tension in the room palpable and electric, like the air before a storm.

"About... us." Daniel's words hung heavy in the air, his expression unreadable as he continued to pack the contents of a nearby bookshelf into yet another box. "I've been doing a lot of thinking lately, and I can't ignore the fact that things have changed between us since Amelia went off to school."

Charlotte felt her heart lurch at his words, fear and sadness creeping up her spine as she tried to process what was happening. She had known that their relationship had been strained the past year, but the reality of the situation was suddenly crashing down upon her like a tidal wave. They hadn't been fighting—was there someone else?

"Changed how?" she asked, desperate for some semblance of clarity amidst the swirling chaos of her thoughts.

There was a long pause before Daniel finally spoke again, his voice heavy with resignation. "I don't know, Charlotte. I just… I think we've both lost sight of who we are and what we want from life. I mean, you're a great mom, but other than raising Charlotte—I-I've never seen you excited to do anything."

Anger spiked in her. "That's not fair. I've been by your side since high school! Through college, through moving back to New York, through all the chaos when you started your firm. And I *am* excited to do something. Paint."

"I mean something worthwhile," he said, snorting. "And being the dutiful girlfriend, the dutiful wife, that's not living—that's going along, being a people pleaser. Don't get me wrong. You're right about

14

sticking by me—but I don't want to be married to someone who just stands there, and smiles, and agrees, but has no life of her own."

As she listened to him, his words struck her like a bolt of lightning. For so long, she *had* been a people pleaser, bending over backward to accommodate the needs of others while neglecting her own desires. She had become a passive observer in her own life, watching from the sidelines.

"Isn't that what you do in a relationship, in a family—make sacrifices? Compromise?"

And now that Amelia was off to college, shouldn't that mean that Charlotte had more time to devote to exactly the things he was complaining she lacked? He should be encouraging her, not splitting.

"To the exclusion of everything else? Where is the excitement in that?" he groused.

"Daniel," she murmured, her hands trembling as she reached out to touch a nearby box. "Do you really think this is the answer?"

He looked at her then, something indescribable flickering across his face before he turned away. "I don't know, Charlotte. But I do know that we can't keep going like this. We both deserve better."

And with that, the room fell silent once more, leaving Charlotte to grapple with the enormity of the decision that loomed between them. One he was apparently making without her input.

The dim light filtering through the curtains cast a soft glow on the packed boxes, highlighting the dust motes that danced in the air. Charlotte stood there, her heart lodged in her throat, as she tried to comprehend the reality unfolding before her.

"Daniel," she whispered, her voice barely audible. "What's really going on?"

He looked up from a box he was taping shut, his eyes meeting hers with sadness. "Charlotte, we're stuck. We've been stuck for a while now, and I think it's time we do something about it. No—time I do something."

"Stuck?" she repeated, her mind racing to decipher the meaning behind his words.

"Look at us," he continued, setting down the tape dispenser and gesturing to the room around them. "We've fallen into a rut, and neither of us is truly happy." Daniel sighed, running a hand through his hair. "I think divorce is the best solution, Charlotte. Since Amelia moved out, we've been living two separate lives under the same roof. We deserve better, don't you think?"

15

We deserve better. He kept saying it. As much as she wanted to argue, to fight for their marriage, a part of her knew he was right. The late work dinners, early weekend golf games for Daniel, and Charlotte staying up late painting, only to go to bed long after Daniel had fallen asleep and wake early before him to go jogging—the spark that had once ignited their love had long since faded, leaving only the embers of a relationship built on routine and complacency.

He hadn't even asked her how the swap meet had gone—and she had been so reluctant to share her meeting with Ashwood with him. She blinked back tears, her initial shock giving way to a wave of resignation.

"Maybe you're right," she conceded, her voice cracking under the weight of her emotions. "I guess...we stopped trying, didn't we?"

"Somewhere along the line, yeah," Daniel agreed, his gaze shifting to the floor. "But we can still find happiness, even if it's apart."

Charlotte's hands shook as she picked up a neatly folded shirt from the pile of clothes on the couch, her eyes watering as she carefully placed it in a box. She hadn't even realized she had started helping Daniel pack their life away until she was knee-deep in the familiar routine, her mind numbly working through the motions.

"Are you...sure?" Charlotte asked tentatively, placing another shirt into the box and feeling the soft fabric between her fingers.

"Yes," Daniel said simply, his voice steady and resigned. He continued to wrap their framed photographs in bubble wrap, the sound of crinkling plastic filling the room like a somber soundtrack to their current situation.

They worked in silence, each lost in their thoughts and struggling to come to terms with the reality of what was unfolding before them. The air between them was thick with unspoken words and lingering regrets, but there was also a strange sense of understanding – an acknowledgment that sometimes, even the deepest love could not withstand the erosion of time and complacency. As she slid a stack of books into a box, she thought about how much she had sacrificed for their marriage – what he called people-pleasing, she had thought of as laying aside her dreams, her passions, her very identity, but for the good of them all as a family. So that they could all succeed together— Amelia as she grew, Daniel as his financial advisement firm took off and grew.

Her fingers traced the spine of a sketchbook she hadn't opened in years, its yellowed pages reminding her that she could have spent these

16

years—what had Lillian Ashwood said—becoming exciting. How had Charlotte allowed herself to become so passive, so lost in the shadow of her marriage? And how had that effort now turned into such a negative in the eyes of her husband—not an appreciated choice, but a shortcoming?

Tears welled up in her eyes, but she blinked them away as she continued packing. With every item she placed into the boxes, she felt an odd mixture of fear and liberation. Fear of facing the unknown, of starting anew without the man who had been her partner for a lifetime. And yet, a sense of liberation accompanied it – she would focus on herself, throw herself into her art, and relearn what it meant to be Charlotte *Anderson* once more. The girl before Daniel Moore.

When the last box was sealed, Daniel heaved it into his arms with a strained grunt and cleared his throat. They made their way toward the front door, each step feeling like wading through molasses, thick with unspoken emotions and the weight of finality.

As they reached the door, Daniel paused. He turned to Charlotte, his expression unreadably deep. "I've rented an apartment in Manhattan," he said, his voice steady but his eyes avoiding hers. "It's not far from the office. Makes sense, I guess, for now."

Charlotte nodded, her throat tight. Manhattan – a new life, new beginnings, and a world away from the home they had built together.

"I'll send for the rest of my stuff," Daniel continued, the words seeming to hang in the air between them, heavy and final.

She watched him, a torrent of emotions swirling inside her. This was it. The end of what they had known, the start of what they would have to learn to live without. She should be angry, she should be shouting and raging. But she just felt *numb*.

There was a pause, another silence that seemed to stretch too long, filled with the enormity of what was happening. Then, Daniel looked at her, really looked at her, with a vulnerability that she almost immediately felt manipulated by. "Charlotte," he began, his voice low, "I need you to do something for me. Something I can't do myself."

She met his gaze, steeling herself for what was to come.

"Can you..." He swallowed, his Adam's apple bobbing with the effort. "Can you tell Amelia about us? About the divorce?"

The request hit her like a physical blow. Her breath caught in her throat, the sheer gall of the responsibility of his decision now being passed to her. Charlotte's heart raced, her mind speeding through the implications of this request. To be the bearer of such news to their daughter, to explain the unexplainable, to shoulder not just her own pain but now Amelia's too – it was overwhelming.

The anger she should have felt all along reared its head. "You know, I think you can tell her," Charlotte said, reaching behind him to open the front door. "I wouldn't want to jump in on that little chore just to keep things smooth for you. You know—*people pleasing.*"

Daniel's eyes widened, and then held hers for a moment longer, a silent apology, before he turned away and walked out the door. The door closed with a soft click, a definitive sound that seemed to echo through the now too-quiet house.

Charlotte stood there, alone in the entryway, the weight of the conversation, the weight of what was to come, resting heavily on her shoulders. She realized in that moment that her life was changing, irrevocably and completely. She was no longer just Charlotte, Daniel's wife; Charlotte, Amelia's mother.

So who was she now?

CHAPTER FOUR

Charlotte stood in the empty living room, her eyes gazing at the spot where their wedding picture used to hang. She had waited until Daniel pulled out of the driveway to walk through the house they once shared, now feeling more like a stranger than an occupant. The sound of Roxanne's car pulling up in the driveway was a necessary jolt, dragging Charlotte back from her melancholic thoughts.

"Char!" Roxanne called out as she burst through the front door, a bottle of wine gripped tightly in her hand. Her red heels clicked loudly on the hardwood floor, announcing her presence with every step. "I came as soon as I heard your voicemail."

Charlotte managed a weak smile, grateful for her sister's presence. "Thanks, Rox. I appreciate you being here."

"Always, sis," Roxanne replied, tossing her purse and keys onto the entryway table with a haphazard clatter. "That's what big sisters are for, right? Now let's get down to business." She bustled into the kitchen, her stride full of purpose.

As Charlotte watched her sister rummage through the cabinets for wine glasses, she envied Roxanne's strong personality. Where Charlotte often found herself bending to the will of others, Roxanne seemed incapable of compromise. It was a quality that had carried her far in life and, currently, made her the pillar Charlotte so desperately needed.

"Found them!" Roxanne exclaimed triumphantly, pulling two glasses out and setting them on the island. "Good to know that Daniel left you something, that weasel." With practiced ease, she uncorked the wine and filled both glasses to the brim. "Now, let's sit and have ourselves a proper heart-to-heart."

They settled into the plush armchairs in the living room, the cozy familiarity of the space a subtle salve for Charlotte's wounded heart. The wine was rich and soothing, warming her from the inside out as they sipped in companionable silence.

"Look at us," Roxanne said, her voice tinged with nostalgia. "Two sisters, just like old times, huh?"

"Except now we're adults drinking wine instead of sneaking Dad's beers," Charlotte added, a small chuckle escaping her lips despite the heaviness in her chest.

"Ah, yes," Roxanne agreed, raising her glass in mock-toast. "To growing up and becoming oh-so-wise."

Charlotte clinked her glass against Roxanne's, the sound ringing bittersweet in the stillness of the house.

"Or at least growing up," Charlotte countered.

The warm glow of the living room lamp cast a golden halo around Roxanne's fiery red hair as she leaned forward, concern etched on her expressive face. Charlotte fidgeted with the frayed edge of the throw pillow in her lap, feeling the weight of her sister's gaze, searching for answers. Roxanne was waiting for Charlotte to start the conversation— Charlotte could tell from her expression.

"Rox," Charlotte began, her voice wavering slightly. "Am I... a pushover?"

Roxanne hesitated, and Charlotte could see the internal struggle playing out behind her eyes. She was torn between protecting her sister's feelings and being brutally honest.

"Char, I love you," Roxanne finally said, her tone gentle but firm. "But I have to be truthful with you. Yeah, you've been a pushover at times."

Charlotte's heart sank, even though she had expected the answer. A lump formed in her throat as she fought back the tears that threatened to spill over.

"Damn it," she muttered, blinking away the moisture in her eyes. Roxanne reached out and gave her hand a reassuring squeeze.

"Hey, don't be so hard on yourself," Roxanne urged, her voice full of empathy. "We all have our moments of weakness. Is that why Daniel said he's leaving? That's a thin excuse, if you ask me."

"Thank you, Rox," Charlotte whispered, her grip tightening on her sister's hand. "For being here, and for not sugarcoating the truth. It's exactly what I needed." She took another long sip of wine. "Now, give me examples. Like, I need some concrete points here."

Roxanne leaned back in her chair and crossed her legs. "Remember when we were kids and you'd always let our cousins choose what games to play? You never wanted to make anyone upset, so you'd just go along with whatever they decided."

Charlotte winced at the memory, acknowledging the truth in Roxanne's words. She nodded slowly, prompting her sister to continue.

20

"Or what about that time you worked so hard on that art for kids program for the community center, only to have someone else take credit for it?" Roxanne continued, her voice tinged with anger on her sister's behalf. "You didn't stand up for yourself, Char. You let them walk all over you."

A pang of regret settled in Charlotte's chest, and she bit her lip, trying not to remember the hurt she had felt at the time. But the memories came flooding back, along with the realization that she had allowed herself to be sidelined in her own life far too often.

"And don't even get me started on Daniel," Roxanne added, taking a sip of her wine before setting the glass down with a thud. "He's always been so controlling – deciding where you guys went to college, where you'd live, discouraging you from getting a job, even what friends you could have based on how they made him look. It's like he's been stifling your spirit, Char. He wanted a trophy wife until he didn't."

Charlotte's hand tightened around her wine glass, her knuckles turning white. She couldn't deny the truth in her sister's words. She had always prioritized others' happiness over her own, desperate for approval and terrified of confrontation. But hearing it from Roxanne made her feel exposed, vulnerable.

"Everyone seemed to see it but me," she murmured, a wave of self-doubt crashing over her. "What's wrong with me, Rox?"

"Nothing's wrong with you, Char," Roxanne said firmly, reaching across the table to rest a hand on her sister's arm. "You're just too kind-hearted for your own good sometimes. You think that by giving in and going along with what others want, you're keeping the peace and making everyone happy. But you're only hurting yourself in the end."

Roxanne's voice filled the dimly lit room, her words weaving through the air like threads of a tapestry that was slowly beginning to unravel. Charlotte studied the whirls and patterns in the wooden table between them, searching for clarity amongst the chaos of her thoughts. As Charlotte listened to her sister's words, she felt grateful for Roxanne's honesty and support, but ashamed that she hadn't recognized her own worth and stood up for herself sooner.

"Think about Amelia's graduation party," Roxanne continued, her tone gentle but insistent. "After you'd planned the whole thing and made sure things went off without a hitch, you spent the entire day running around, catering to everyone else's needs, making sure they were comfortable—that the music was okay, or that the gluten-free options were okay. Even though Amelia kept trying to get you to sit

21

down, you barely even took a moment to enjoy your own daughter's accomplishment."

Charlotte winced as the memory surfaced, her heart clenching with regret. She hadn't realized it at the time, but she had been so focused on pleasing everyone that she'd failed to truly be present for one of the most important days of her child's life. And wasn't that the ultimate irony? Her desire to make others happy had only left her feeling empty and disconnected.

She took a shaky breath, forcing herself to meet her sister's gaze. "I never meant to be this way, Rox," she admitted, the words tasting like ash on her tongue. "I just... I don't know how to change. How do I stop letting people walk all over me without becoming someone I'm not? I don't want to be some cold witch who has no regard for anyone else's feelings."

An image of Lillian Ashwood flashed in Charlotte's mind.

Roxanne's eyes were warm and understanding. "You're an incredible artist, Char. You have this amazing gift for creating beauty out of nothing, for seeing the world in a way that no one else does. You need to channel that same energy into standing up for yourself."

The tension within Charlotte grew, a battle raging deep inside her soul. She longed to embrace some newfound sense of agency, to finally break free from the chains of her people-pleasing tendencies. But the thought of disappointing or upsetting those she cared about made her stomach twist into knots.

Except Daniel—as she took another sip of wine, she thought of all the ways she hoped he was upset in the near future. She hoped all of his shoelaces snapped right as he was running late for work. She hoped that he caught several colds. She hoped that if he ever tried to date again, he got incurable, severe dandruff.

But everyone else—like Roxanne, like Amelia?

"Is it really so bad to want to make others happy?" Charlotte asked, her voice barely a whisper.

"Of course not," Roxanne reassured her, giving her arm a comforting squeeze. "But there's a difference between being kind and being a doormat, Char. You have to learn how to strike that balance, to find your own happiness without sacrificing yourself in the process."

Charlotte's eyes welled up with tears as she studied the delicate lines of her sister's face. Roxanne's strong, steady gaze seemed to anchor her amidst the storm of emotions that threatened to sweep her away. A tear slid down Charlotte's cheek, leaving a warm trail in its wake as it landed on her hand. She clenched her fingers into a fist.

"Remember when we were kids, Char?" Roxanne asked, a wistful smile playing on her lips. "We used to build forts out of blankets and pretend we were fearless adventurers, ready to conquer the world."

"Of course," Charlotte replied, a bittersweet nostalgia settling over her. "But that bravery doesn't feel real anymore."

"Maybe not," Roxanne acknowledged, her eyes sparkling with determination. "But that's the thing about bravery – it's not something you're born with. It's something you choose every single day. You can recapture that. Daniel might have made the most loser decision of his life, but he hasn't taken away your ability to get through the fallout. I say, if he wants you to be miserable, you do the opposite—go out and live it up. Be as happy as you can be. Show him that your life can be better without him, just like he's insisting."

Charlotte looked deep into her sister's eyes, feeling a flicker of hope ignite within her chest. She knew Roxanne was right; she had the power to reshape her own story and redefine herself.

"What about painting full-time?" Roxanne ventured, her voice laced with genuine curiosity.

The question made Charlotte pause, her heart skipping a beat at the prospect. Could she really do that? Was it possible to build a life around what truly brought her joy? Her thoughts raced, fueled by the potency of the wine and the encouragement from her sister.

"Maybe," Charlotte whispered, the word tasting like possibility on her lips. She almost told Roxanne about the rejection from Ashwood. But then, louder, instead, she said, "You know—yes!"

"Darn right, it's time!" Roxanne cheered, raising her glass in a toast.

The night wore on, and as the wine continued to flow, so did their conversation. And maybe it was her sister's encouragement, and maybe it was the wine, but Charlotte felt a shift within herself. She was no longer just a bystander in her own story. She was the protagonist, ready to take control of the narrative and paint a new future.

She would start tomorrow. Tonight was for letting loose with Roxanne.

CHAPTER FIVE

Later that evening, the front door clicked shut behind Charlotte as she leaned against it. Her breathing was labored, and her head was spinning from the wine. The house was silent, and now that Roxanne had left, Daniel's absence was palpable. The emptiness weighed on Charlotte like a thick fog.

"Darn it," she muttered under her breath, wiping away tears with the back of her hand. Her swollen eyes searched for a distraction, anything to keep her mind off the sudden upheaval that had shattered her life like fragile porcelain. It was hard to ignore without the vibrant presence of her sister to distract her.

Charlotte's gaze fell upon a dusty box in the corner of the living room, something Daniel must have unearthed while he'd packed. Curious, Charlotte approached the box, noting the letters "A" and "R" written on the side – her maiden initials. She knelt, her fingers trembling as they traced the familiar, faded ink. She hesitated, her heart pounding in her chest, before tugging at the tape sealing the box shut.

As she lifted the cardboard flaps, a musty smell wafted up, tinged with memories of a time long gone. She rummaged through the contents: a collection of sketchbooks, a few old paintbrushes, and other dried-out art supplies. Beneath them lay a small stack of photographs, each one a frozen moment from her past. She picked one up cautiously, and a wave of nostalgia washed over her.

"Wow," she breathed, staring at the image. It was a photograph of her, Roxanne, and their dad, Henry, all smiling brightly. They appeared younger, carefree, and blissfully unaware of the challenges that lay ahead. Charlotte could almost hear her sister's sassy laughter echoing through the years, a sound that always managed to bring a smile to her face.

"Rox, Dad," she murmured, the memories seeping into her thoughts like ink on paper. The photo had captured a moment in time that felt both distant and achingly close – a reminder of what once was, and what could have been. Charlotte's fingers lingered on the photograph, her eyes drawn to their surroundings in the image. They had been standing on a rocky beach, windblown hair framing their smiling faces, while waves crashed behind them. She closed her eyes and breathed deeply, as if she could still smell the salty air. The memory of that summer vacation to Chesham Cove, England, came flooding back to her.

"Come on, girls!" their dad had called out, waving them toward the shore. *"The water's perfect!"*

Charlotte shook herself from the remembrance, tears pricking at the corners of her eyes. That summer had been magical – a time when laughter came easily, and happiness felt like an endless horizon stretched out before them.

Things were so simple back then, Charlotte thought, her heart aching with longing for the past. *Everything was so different.* She thought of her life now – the empty house, Daniel's absence, and her faltering career as an artist. It seemed like a cruel contrast to the joy she had once known. As Charlotte continued to gaze at the photo, she felt a growing doggedness within her. She couldn't change the past, but as Roxanne had said, she could take control of her future. The carefree girl on that rocky beach, with her entire life ahead of her, was still there – buried beneath years of heartache and disappointment.

"Maybe Chesham Cove holds the key to finding myself again," Charlotte murmured, tracing the edges of the photograph. Her mother had been the one to snap the photo, and now Charlotte recalled the weeks following their mother's funeral, so many years later, the house heavy with grief and emptiness. Her art school acceptance letter had arrived just days before, but she couldn't bring herself to feel excitement amidst the sorrow.

And then, Henry Anderson had just disappeared. Poof. Packed some things, much like Daniel, and gone from her life and Rox's. The memory of her father's absence stirred a deep ache within her, one that had never fully faded. They had been left to pick up the pieces, Roxanne inheriting the responsibility of their family home while Charlotte pursued her dreams of becoming an artist—and molded herself into the box that Daniel built for them.

The memories of the bliss she'd felt at Chesham Cove came flooding back as Charlotte stared once more at the worn photograph. She could almost feel the cool breeze that had danced along the coast, carrying the scent of salt and seaweed. The sun had been warm on her skin that day as she'd stood between her sister and their father, all three of them grinning with pure joy. It was there, in that quaint little village nestled along the cliffs, that she had last felt truly happy. A time before loss and heartache had become constant companions.

Her head swam with all the wine she'd had. She hiccupped softly as she stared at the photo.

"Maybe I'll find a little cottage near the shore," she mused, picking up her glass and sipping her wine again. "I could paint in the mornings, listening to the seagulls and the waves crashing against the rocks."

She envisioned herself walking through the cobbled streets of the quaint town, exchanging pleasantries with friendly locals and discovering hidden gems to paint, tucked away in the vibrant landscape.

"I could even teach art classes," she continued, "Or hold exhibitions at a local gallery. Open *my own gallery*. To heck with you, *Ashwood Fine Arts!* I'll even have a fling with a sexy British guy. A duke. A baron."

"Roxanne will be so surprised when I tell her," she whispered, hiccupping again, her eyes sparkling with excitement at the thought of her sister's reaction. Charlotte stood and wobbled to the side table where she'd left her phone, setting down her wine glass and swiping to wake her screen.

She began texting furiously, her confidence in her plans for the future growing with every word that appeared on the phone screen. Yes, this was all just perfect. The perfect plan. Nothing could go wrong.

CHAPTER SIX

Late morning light pierced the curtains as Charlotte stirred in her bed, feeling groggy and disoriented. The taste of stale alcohol lingered in her mouth, and she blinked several times, trying to shake off the haze that clouded her mind. Last night's drinking session with Roxanne had been a much-needed escape from the cold, hard reality of her crumbling marriage. Yet now, as her head throbbed and her vision swam, she regretted the last *several* glasses.

"Ugh," she muttered, rubbing her temples and propping herself up on her elbows. The room seemed to tilt and sway around her, fragments of memories from the previous night floating in and out of her consciousness like ghosts. As an artist, Charlotte was no stranger to the allure of escapism, but today it felt more like a cruel joke than a comfort.

Suddenly, her phone rang from somewhere amidst the tangled sheets, its shrill tone jarring her back to full awareness. She fumbled blindly for the device, her heart pounding in sudden panic.

"Hello?" she croaked, her voice barely recognizable through the fog of her hangover.

"Charlotte, is that you?" The voice on the other end of the line sounded concerned, yet oddly familiar. "It's Helen from the bank. I've been trying to reach you all morning! Are you all right?"

The concern in the voice momentarily pulled Charlotte out of her confusion. It was comforting to know someone cared—even if it was only her favorite bank teller, and even if everything else seemed to be falling apart.

"Yeah, fine. I—why are you calling? I'm sorry, it's just unusual…"

"Charlotte, I'm sorry to tell you this, but Daniel has emptied your joint bank accounts," Helen said, her tone grave and urgent. "I just froze. Another teller had to help him. I got a bad feeling when you weren't there."

"Wh-what?" Charlotte stuttered, her heart skipping a beat. The fog in her head lifted for a brief moment as panic surged through her veins. Her grip tightened around the phone, knuckles turning white with tension. "That can't be right. There must be some mistake."

"There's no mistake. I've checked and double-checked the records. Everything is gone," Helen replied, apologetic and solemn.

Charlotte's chest constricted, making it difficult to breathe. She sank back into the pillows, feeling like she had just been punched in the gut. Waves of panic washed over her, followed by an overwhelming sense of disbelief. How could Daniel have done something so cruel and heartless? They had built their lives together—he had said himself that she'd been by his side without fail—and now he was ripping it all away from her without a second thought.

As the reality of her situation began to sink in, Charlotte felt a cold dread creeping up her spine, settling in the pit of her stomach like a lead weight. With the joint accounts drained, she would struggle to pay the bills, let alone maintain her life. And how could she start painting full-time without money? She had a small nest egg, but that would quickly run out.

Tears prickled at the corners of her eyes as her vision blurred. Her throat tightened, and she swallowed hard, trying to choke back the sob that threatened to escape her lips. "I-I don't understand," she whispered, her voice barely audible. "How could he do this to me?"

Helen hesitated, sympathy evident in every word. "I don't know, Charlotte. But I have to go. I could get in trouble for even calling you now."

Charlotte nodded, as though Helen could see her, her throat still too tight for words. She swallowed several times until she could speak. "Thanks, Helen."

She hung up the phone and took a deep breath. She couldn't afford to wallow in self-pity any longer – not when her entire life was at stake. Her future depended on her ability to act quickly and decisively, even if it meant stepping out of her comfort zone.

"Alright," she murmured to herself, grabbing a notebook and pen from the bedside table and fighting the nausea that rose from her impressive hangover. "Let's start with finding a job." She began scribbling down ideas, listing possible opportunities and connections. As an artist, she knew it wouldn't be easy to secure a stable income, but she was willing to do whatever it took to regain control over her life. She could work an office job, or even wait tables.

Charlotte's phone buzzed on the bed, interrupting her train of thought. Picking it up, she saw a flight alert notification flashing on the screen: *Flight BA219 to London Heathrow departing at 1:00 p.m.*

today. Digital check-in available. Please click here when you arrive at the gate.

"Wait, what?" Charlotte blinked in surprise, not recalling having booked a flight at all. Last night's drunken haze had left her memory foggy, but as she stared at the notification, fragments of recollection swirled within her mind. A conversation with Roxanne about starting fresh, the picture of Chesham Cove, a spontaneous decision to book a ticket. It seemed too surreal to be true, yet there it was, in plain text on her screen.

"London?" she whispered. For a moment, she considered ignoring the notification and carrying on with her efforts to find a job. But as she gazed at the words *London Heathrow* for a few seconds more, an idea began to blossom in her mind. Charlotte couldn't deny the allure of the opportunity that lay before her. She had a flight booked and paid for— and as she checked her email for the payment confirmation, it seemed that she'd bought the ticket with money from the joint account before Daniel had cleaned it out. Now, with nothing left to lose, the prospect of leaving behind the remnants of her failed marriage seemed more and more enticing.

Charlotte's fingers hovered over the screen, trembling with uncertainty. It was as if there was a fierce internal battle taking place between her fear of the unknown and the longing for change. Her heart thudded in her chest, beating out a rhythm that echoed the words "London" and "Heathrow" in her mind.

"Roxanne always said I should travel more," she muttered to herself, grasping at any reason to make this sudden, impulsive decision feel right. What was stopping her from going to England to find a job and start anew? If she failed, she'd just come home after a couple weeks to no worse a situation than she left.

Charlotte tossed her phone onto the bed and sprang into reasonable-for-being-hungover action. She yanked open the closet door, grabbing clothes haphazardly and stuffing them into her suitcase. She almost smiled at how easy it was to get her luggage out now that Daniel's wasn't taking up space at the top of the closet. The sound of fabric rustling and zippers being pulled filled the room, drowning out the lingering doubts that still tried to take hold of her.

"London, here I come," she declared. A pair of jeans landed on the bed beside her phone, followed by a handful of shirts, underwear, and socks. Each item added propelled her to move faster, more decisively.

"Passport, wallet, toothbrush," she muttered under her breath like a mantra, ensuring she had everything she needed for the journey ahead. Time seemed to slip away from her, each tick of the clock only adding to the growing sense of urgency within her. It was nine now—the flight reminder had said takeoff at one. She could exchange currency when she arrived, and her cell phone had a plan that allowed international... She was sure she could figure out the details on the way. People had been travelling abroad for much longer—and in far less digital eras—than Charlotte.

Finally, with her suitcase filled to the brim, Charlotte took a shaky breath and zipped it closed. She glanced around the room one last time, taking in the life she was about to leave behind. Her eyes lingered on the now-empty closet, the hastily-made bed, and the phone still displaying that fateful flight alert.

"Goodbye, old life," she murmured. And with a final deep breath, Charlotte grabbed her suitcase and strode purposefully toward the door, ready to embrace whatever awaited her across the ocean.

Charlotte's hand trembled as she locked the front door behind her. She hesitated for a moment, staring at the familiar chipped paint on the doorjamb, a door that had once welcomed her into a home full of love and laughter. Now, it was just a symbol of what used to be.

"England, here I come," she said with more confidence, summoning every ounce of courage she possessed.

CHAPTER SEVEN

With her heart pounding, Charlotte approached the security checkpoint. The airport's familiar hum of announcements and distant chatter did nothing to quell her nerves as the line inched forward. She held her ID tightly in her shaky hands, her artist's fingers more accustomed to gripping a paintbrush than navigating the complexities of air travel.

"Next," called out the security officer, his expression bored yet attentive.

"Hello," Charlotte managed, swallowing hard as she handed over her documents.

"Charlotte Moore?" he asked, studying her ID and then looking up at her with scrutinizing eyes.

"Yes," she replied, trying to keep her voice steady. *Anderson*, she wanted to say, but that would come soon enough.

"Place your items in the bin and step through the scanner, please," he instructed, handing back her documents.

Charlotte complied, placing her purse and cell phone into one of the gray bins and removing her shoes – a pair of well-worn flats. As she stepped through the scanner, she felt exposed, every inch of her being examined by the unseen inner workings of the machine. When the scanner beeped its approval, she let out a breath she hadn't realized she'd been holding.

"Thank you," she mumbled, gathering her belongings and slipping her feet back into her shoes. The security checkpoint now behind her, Charlotte focused on finding her gate amidst the maze of airport corridors.

"Gate B22," she muttered under her breath, scanning the signs overhead before spotting her destination. Her steps became more confident as she weaved through the bustling crowd.

When she reached the departure gate, she stood at the window, her heart pounding in sync with the rhythmic ticking of the airport's massive clock. The bustling crowd of travelers around her blurred into a cacophony of noise as she stared at her phone, the barcode of her digital boarding pass to London, the device feeling foreign in her trembling hands. She exhaled slowly, her breath fogging up the glass window that separated her from the airplane on the tarmac. Her chest tightened with uncertainty, and she contemplated whether to turn back.

She glanced down at her suddenly buzzing phone. It was Amelia.

Oh, shoot. Before the whole drama with Daniel, Charlotte had told her daughter she would call—and she hadn't. She answered, trying to sound cheerful.

"What's going on? Where are you?"

"Hi, sweetie," Charlotte said, trying to steady her voice. "I'm... I'm at the airport."

"Airport?" Amelia sounded surprised. "You never told me you were going anywhere. What's happening? You said you would call yesterday after the swap meet."

Charlotte hesitated, gripping the phone tightly. "The swap meet was good. I sold two paintings." She hesitated. "I'm going to London," she finally revealed.

"London?" Amelia exclaimed, excitement bubbling through the line. "That's amazing, Mom! But why? Is this a spontaneous trip or something?"

"Something like that," Charlotte replied quietly, glancing around the busy terminal. The truth felt too heavy to unload onto Amelia just yet. And obviously Daniel hadn't bothered to tell their daughter, yet. "It's been a long time since I've had an adventure. And I think it's time for a new one. Besides, I'm bored without you around, kiddo."

"Wow," Amelia marveled, her voice full of enthusiasm. "This is so unexpected, but I'm so excited for you, Mom. You deserve this!"

Charlotte's eyes welled up with tears, touched by her daughter's excitement. She knew Amelia was right; she did deserve this. And with her daughter's voice in her ear, the uncertainty that had gripped her heart began to fade.

"Thank you, sweetie," Charlotte whispered, her voice filled with gratitude. "I'll call you as soon as I land, okay?"

"Sounds good," Amelia chirped. "Have a safe flight, Mom. Love you!"

"Love you too, Amelia." Charlotte took a deep breath and clutched her phone tighter. Taking a deep breath, Charlotte hesitated for a moment before deciding to open up to Amelia. "Wait. Don't hang up. Honey, there's something I need to tell you before I go," she said softly, her voice wavering with the weight of the news. "Your father... he left me."

"Wait, what?!" Amelia's shock was palpable, and Charlotte could practically see her daughter's wide blue eyes through the phone.

"Daniel took all our money and left," Charlotte continued, trying to keep her composure. "But don't worry. I made sure your college savings are safe." She hoped that small reassurance would be enough to alleviate some of Amelia's concern.

"Mom, that's... that's awful," Amelia stammered, clearly taken aback by the unexpected revelation. "Dad is so wrong for doing this to you. Does he—is there some other woman?"

Charlotte pinched the bridge of her nose. "I don't think so, honey."

"He didn't answer my call a few minutes ago. I bet he's avoiding me. How could he do this? I swear, I'm going to blow up his phone and texts until he explains—"

The reflection of the departure gate lights shimmered in the pools of tears that clung to Charlotte's eyelashes, even as she laughed at her daughter's vehemence.

"No, no. Just leave him be for now. You have class all week."

Amelia sighed over the line. "Fine. I'll just ignore his calls if he tries me."

Charlotte took a slow, calming breath as she tried to channel her daughter's strength.

"Final boarding call to London," echoed the overhead announcement, drawing Charlotte's attention.

"Amelia, I love you," she said into the phone, her voice thick with emotion. "I'll call you as soon as I land."

"Love you too, Mom," Amelia replied softly, a hint of fierceness still present in her tone.

Charlotte disconnected the call and slipped her phone into her purse, then hesitated for a moment. Her heart raced as she stared at the open door leading to the jet bridge. The decision felt monumental – a single step that would irrevocably change her life. She joined the queue and waited impatiently for her turn to board the plane – the vessel that would carry her away from the life she'd known and toward the unknown future that awaited her in London.

"Welcome aboard, Ms. Moore," the flight attendant greeted her as she stepped onto the plane, studying her boarding pass before gesturing down the aisle. "Your seat is 23A."

"Thank you," Charlotte replied, her voice barely audible above the din of settling passengers.

Navigating the cramped space, she finally arrived at her window seat. With a sigh of relief, she stowed her purse beneath the seat in front of her and settled into the embrace of the airplane chair. As she fastened her seatbelt, Charlotte's hands shook slightly – a mix of nervousness and anticipation coursing through her veins. She could hardly believe that she was actually doing this – going on an adventure to a foreign land, a world away from the shattered remnants of her life in New York.

"Everything okay?" asked the woman sitting beside her, noticing the tremble in Charlotte's hands.

"Ah, yes," Charlotte assured her, offering a small smile. "Just a bit nervous, I suppose."

"First time flying alone?" the woman inquired sympathetically.

"Something like that," Charlotte admitted with a soft laugh.

The plane's engines roared to life, vibrating through the cabin as they prepared for takeoff. Charlotte glanced out of the window, her eyes fixed on the tarmac outside. She felt the sensation of her stomach lurching forward as the jet picked up speed, and she gripped the armrests tightly.

"Here we go," she whispered to herself, feeling a mixture of exhilaration and fear.

As the aircraft ascended, Charlotte watched the cityscape of New York shrink beneath them, its towering skyscrapers receding into the distance like toys abandoned by a careless giant. The clouds swallowed the city whole, leaving nothing but an endless expanse of white fluff in their wake.

What it looked like to Charlotte was exactly what she needed—a clean slate. A blank canvas.

CHAPTER EIGHT

A wave of anticipation washed over Charlotte as the plane touched down at London's Heathrow Airport. She took a deep breath, feeling the weight of her old life waiting to be left behind. The gentle hum of fellow passengers unbuckling their seatbelts and gathering their belongings blended with the rhythmic footsteps of flight attendants moving up and down the aisle.

"Thank you for flying with us," one of the flight attendants said, smiling warmly at Charlotte as she stepped into the bustling airport terminal. Her heart fluttered at the thought of the adventure that awaited her in this foreign city.

Locating the baggage claim area, Charlotte weaved her way through the sea of travelers, her eyes scanning the conveyor belt for her suitcase. With each passing moment, the familiar artistic energy that coursed through her veins grew more potent. She knew that London's rich history and enchanting scenery would serve as the perfect muse for her art. She could paint here—she could feel it in her bones.

"Ah, there it is," Charlotte murmured softly to herself as she spotted her teal suitcase. Lifting it off the conveyor belt, she slung her well-loved leather satchel over her shoulder and made her way to the exit.

The cool London air nipped gently at Charlotte's cheeks as she stepped outside, the sun casting long shadows across the pavement. She hailed a taxi, the vibrant yellow car pulling up before her with a satisfying crunch of gravel. The driver, a middle-aged man with silver hair, adjusted the rearview mirror as Charlotte settled in the backseat.

"Where to, love?" he asked, his voice and accent wrapping around Charlotte like a comforting embrace.

"Um, the train station, please," Charlotte replied, her fingers absentmindedly tracing the address on a crumpled piece of paper. She read it off, and he nodded. "But, um, could you drive around a bit first, please? I'd like to see some of the city."

"Righto," the driver said cheerfully, shifting the taxi into gear and pulling away from the curb. As they navigated through London's bustling streets, Charlotte marveled at the city's unique blend of historic charm and vibrant modernity. The artist in her longed to capture its essence within her work, the colors and textures begging to be immortalized on canvas.

"London's quite the sight, isn't it?" the driver commented, catching Charlotte's gaze in the mirror as she snapped a few photos with her phone camera. She nodded, her eyes sparkling with excitement.

"Indeed," Charlotte replied, her voice barely audible as her thoughts drifted toward Chesham Cove.

Charlotte's heart pounded in her chest as the taxi driver expertly maneuvered through the busy streets of London. The iconic landmarks she'd seen only in movies and postcards now stood before her, tangible and breathtaking. Big Ben loomed proudly in the distance, its clock face a sentinel over the city, while the grand structure of the London Eye traced an arc against the sky.

"Our famous sights," the driver remarked, his gaze flicking to Charlotte's reflection in the rearview mirror as she stared in wonder at the passing scenery.

"Everything's so beautiful," she murmured, her voice filled with awe. "I've always dreamed of visiting London."

"First time here, then?" he asked, skillfully navigating around a double-decker bus.

"Yes, unfortunately," Charlotte admitted, shifting her focus from the stunning cityscape to the people walking by on the crowded sidewalks. Their distinct British accents floated into the open window of the taxi, weaving a melodic tapestry.

"Really? Well, you picked a fine city to start with. London has a lot to offer, especially for someone like yourself," the driver said warmly, sensing Charlotte's appreciation for the beauty around her.

"Someone like me?" she queried, her curiosity piqued.

"An artist," he replied. "Ain't ya? You've got paint on your sleeve, love, and that look in your eye. There's inspiration everywhere you look."

Charlotte smiled, touched by the driver's insight. "You're absolutely right," she agreed, her fingers itching to pick up a paintbrush and capture the unique essence of London – the fusion of old and new, the vibrant energy pulsating through its very core. "I'll be heading to Chesham Cove soon," she shared, a sense of longing filling her chest as she thought about the quaint coastal village that awaited her.

"Ah, Chesham Cove. A lovely place, that is," he nodded knowingly. "I'm sure you'll find plenty of inspiration there, too."

As the taxi made its way across a bridge spanning the River Thames, Charlotte found herself captivated by the scene unfolding around her. Street artists adorned the sidewalks, their hands moving deftly as they added vibrant swaths of color to their latest masterpieces. The sounds of street performers – a saxophonist's dulcet tones, the rhythmic beat of a drummer, and someone singing along with an acoustic guitar – melded together into a symphony that seemed to be London's very heartbeat.

"Wow," she murmured, entranced by the energy pulsating through the bustling crowds.

"Would you like me to stop, miss?" the driver asked, noticing her fascination.

"Please," she replied, already reaching for her phone.

The taxi pulled over, and Charlotte stepped out onto the sidewalk, eager to immerse herself in the sensory feast laid before her. With practiced ease, she adjusted the settings on her phone camera, capturing the intricate details of the street art – the way the colors blended seamlessly together, the emotions etched into each stroke.

"Amazing, isn't it?" a passerby remarked, pausing beside her to admire the artwork.

"Absolutely," Charlotte agreed, grateful for a moment of connection. "I can't wait to paint some of these scenes when I get back to my studio."

With a final click of her camera, Charlotte turned back toward the waiting taxi, her heart lighter than it had been in months. There was no one who expected her to be anywhere or do anything right now—there was only this fascinating new place where no one knew her or had any preconceived notions about her.

The taxi dropped her at the station, and Charlotte paid and tipped generously—courtesy of a stash of cash that she had found in a pair of shoes that Daniel had left behind, a stash that she had happily taken. The train station was abuzz with life, a microcosm of London's energetic pulse. Charlotte made her way through the throngs of people, their laughter and conversations blending into an indistinguishable hum. The scent of fresh beef pasties from a nearby café intermingled with the distinct aroma of diesel, creating a peculiar yet comforting olfactory blend.

"Excuse me," she said to the woman at the ticket counter, "I'd like a ticket to Chesham Cove, please."

"Ah, a lovely little place," the attendant replied with a warm smile, handing over the ticket. "Enjoy your journey!"

"Thank you," Charlotte murmured, clutching the small paper rectangle that represented her rebirth.

Boarding the train, she found an empty window seat and settled in, her fingers still tracing the edges of the ticket. She gazed out as the cityscape began to blur, the train picking up speed and leaving behind the cacophony of urban life. As the landscape transformed from concrete jungle to picturesque countryside, Charlotte felt the weight of her heartache ease ever so slightly. As the train sped along, Charlotte found herself utterly captivated by the ever-changing landscape outside her window. The hustle and bustle of London had been replaced with a serene expanse of rolling hills, their verdant slopes dotted with grazing sheep. The scene was like a watercolor painting come to life, and her artist's eye reveled in the vibrant hues and subtle textures that unfolded before her.

"Look at that village," Charlotte murmured to herself, leaning closer to the glass as they passed by a cluster of quaint cottages nestled amidst lush gardens. Each home boasted a unique charm, with ivy-covered walls, thatched roofs, and intricate woodwork.

The train rounded a bend, and suddenly the coastline came into view. Charlotte caught her breath at the sight: a dazzling expanse of azure sea met a horizon that seemed to stretch on forever. Ochre cliffs loomed over hidden coves, and gulls cried out as they wheeled above the frothy waves. Charlotte's heart swelled with anticipation and a quiet sense of hope. She turned back to the window, watching intently as the train carried her closer to the place that would become her sanctuary, her muse, and perhaps even her salvation.

CHAPTER NINE

Raindrops fell with a rhythmic patter on the cobblestone streets of Chesham Cove, creating a soggy symphony that accompanied Charlotte's arrival in the dreary coastal town. The dense fog enshrouded the imposing cliffs that loomed in the near distance, casting a somber shadow over the small fishing village. An icy gust of wind sent a shiver down her spine as she stepped onto the slick stones before her.

"Must be quite the storm coming," Charlotte muttered to herself, pulling her coat closer and adjusting the scarf around her neck. Thank goodness she had packed for all weather possibilities—because she had not expected this. She had hoped for a more welcoming atmosphere upon her arrival, but the gloomy weather seemed intent on setting a different tone.

As she walked through the narrow streets, she couldn't help but notice the curious glances cast her way by the locals. Huddled beneath their umbrellas or taking shelter under awnings, they whispered amongst themselves as they eyed her unfamiliar face. Their stares left Charlotte feeling exposed, like a lone tree in a barren field, its branches stripped bare by winter winds.

"New around here, are you?" an elderly woman called from a corner shop, her voice suspicious. Charlotte nodded in affirmation, sensing the veiled inquiry behind the simple question.

"From London, actually," Charlotte offered, attempting to quell some of the curiosity that seemed to cling to her like the rain-soaked fabric of her coat. "Just needed a change of scenery."

The woman's eyes narrowed as if she were weighing the merits of Charlotte's explanation. "Keep your wits about you, dearie."

What does that mean? Was that a threat?

Charlotte dropped her gaze and hurried along the side of the cobblestone street. She had to find The Crown Inn—the other drunken booking she had made that night. She swallowed hard, fighting back the unease that threatened to consume her. She couldn't explain why the woman's words had unsettled her, but she couldn't shake the feeling that they were at least partially true. She would need to have her wits about her here.

Maybe they're not used to outsiders, Charlotte thought as she walked, trying to make sense of her growing discomfort. *Or maybe it's just my nerves playing tricks on me.*

The rain continued to fall around her, droplets leaving their mark on the cobblestones beneath her feet – a subtle reminder that, for better or worse, her journey had solidly begun. Only it seemed more *Sleet, Gray, Mud* than *Eat, Pray, Love.*

With each step closer to The Crown Inn, Charlotte's anticipation grew. She recalled the charming building she had seen on the website when booking her stay. Nestled between two towering oak trees and adorned with ivy creeping up its brick walls, the inn website had promised a warmth and coziness that she longed for after her cold, damp journey.

"Only a few more streets to go," she murmured to herself, her breath fogging up in the chilly air. At least, that's what her phone GPS said. As she ventured deeper into Chesham Cove, Charlotte began to notice the quaint downtown area coming alive around her.

"Fresh fish, get your fresh fish here!" shouted a burly man from a nearby stall, his voice carrying over the sound of the raindrops splattering against the awnings of shops lining the cobblestone street. The scent of freshly baked bread wafted out from a bakery, tempting her with the promise of warm, buttery pastries.

Ooh, I'll have to remember this place later, she thought, making a mental note of the tiny shop's location.

Despite the dreary weather, Charlotte was captivated by the charm and character of Chesham Cove. The unique shops, their windows filled with colorful trinkets and handmade crafts, seemed to beckon her inside as if they held secrets waiting to be discovered.

"Would you like an umbrella, miss?" a young girl asked, shyly holding up an array of brightly colored umbrellas outside a small store. "You look like you could use one."

"Thank you, dear," Charlotte replied with a grateful smile, selecting a deep purple umbrella that seemed to match the hue of the stormy sky overhead. She handed the girl a few bills before continuing on her way.

See? That was a positive. Mustn't let the rain dampen my spirits, she thought, hoisting her new umbrella above her head and reveling in the simple pleasure of its shelter. Then, her phone made a beep, and the GPS rerouted, telling her that The Crown Inn was the exact *opposite* direction of where she was currently.

Luckily, she spotted the pub just ahead: The Laughing Lobster. Its quirky exterior featured a hand-painted sign with a grinning crustacean holding a pint of beer in one claw. Ivy climbed up the walls, framing the leaded glass windows that gave way to warm, golden light spilling onto the sidewalk.

"Must be fate," Charlotte thought as she pushed open the heavy wooden door, feeling a rush of warmth and good cheer envelop her. The lively atmosphere inside was contagious – laughter echoed off the walls, and the friendly banter between patrons created a sense of camaraderie that made her feel welcome.

"Evening," greeted the bartender, his eyes twinkling with curiosity. "You must be the new chickie in town."

"Am I that obvious?" Charlotte asked with a chuckle, taking a seat at the bar and parking her rolling suitcase next to her.

"Word travels fast in Chesham Cove," he replied, pouring her a pint of their local ale. "It's not every day we get newcomers around here. Here. On the house."

She accepted the drink gratefully. "I'm looking for directions to The Crown Inn."

He pulled a face that made her frown. "Is there something wrong with The Crown Inn?"

"Nothing wrong, per se," he answered, leaning in conspiratorially. "It's just...well, it has a bit of history to it, if you catch my drift."

"History? What kind of history?" Charlotte's interest was piqued, her fingers tapping against the cool glass of her pint.

"It's old," he teased, winking at her. "Surprised the building still stands, to be honest. But don't worry. Margaret's, the owner, is a fine gal. For now, enjoy your drink and the company. When you're done, I'll point you there."

As Charlotte sipped her ale, she eavesdropped on the conversations around her. The locals were clearly intrigued by her presence, exchanging whispers and curious glances in her direction. She found it oddly endearing.

After she finished her pint, the bartender gave her a detailed set of instructions that she committed to memory.

"Head down the main street until you reach the old stone bridge. Cross it, then take the second left onto Rosemary Lane. Follow it as it curves around the park, and you'll find The Crown Inn tucked away on the corner."

"Thank you," Charlotte replied gratefully, her anticipation building at the thought of finally reaching her destination.

Stepping back out into the cool evening air, Charlotte followed the bartender's directions through the winding streets of Chesham Cove. Each step brought her closer to the place she would call home for the next few weeks.

As she reached the old stone bridge, Charlotte noticed a small path leading down to the harbor. Her curiosity got the better of her, and she decided to take a detour. The picturesque view was too inviting to ignore – the sea stretched out before her, its surface shimmering under the moonlight. Fishing boats bobbed gently in the water, their colorful hulls casting vibrant reflections on the waves.

"Wow," she whispered, her breath catching at the sight.

It had been years since she'd been this close to the ocean, and the salty breeze stirred something within her – an inexplicable sense of peace. It was hard to believe that only a few hours earlier, she had been a stranger in this charming corner of the world. Though she couldn't shake off the feeling of being an outsider, there was something about Chesham Cove that made her feel as if she were coming home.

Somewhere here was the exact place where she, Roxanne, and her parents had stood to take that old photo—and Charlotte wanted to find it.

CHAPTER TEN

The sun dipped low in the sky, burning dully through the rain clouds, as Charlotte finally found the spot where the old photograph had been taken. A soft breeze played with her hair, carrying the smell of saltwater and the distant cries of seagulls. The waves crashed against the rocky coastline, their white foam contrasting vividly with the dark stones.

"Roxanne would love this," she murmured to herself, thinking of her sister's affinity for beautiful landscapes. Charlotte's landscapes were what Roxanne always cooed over.

There was a group of fishermen docked nearby, but she couldn't imagine asking the any of the brawny outdoorsman to take her picture, and so Charlotte carefully pulled out her phone and glanced at the photograph again, comparing it to the scene before her. The viewpoint was perfect, capturing Chesham Cove's wild beauty.

"Let's see if I can do this justice," Charlotte said resolutely, adjusting the settings on her phone. She scanned the area for a suitable spot to prop up her phone, her artist's eye searching for the right angle and composition.

Spying a flat rock nearby, she placed her phone on it, using her phone stand and some small pebbles to angle it just right. The wind picked up slightly, making her shiver in damp coat, but she smiled at the thought of sharing this moment with her sister. She knew that the photograph would make Roxanne smile—especially since she had no idea yet that Charlotte was halfway around the world.

"Okay, let's do this," Charlotte whispered to herself, taking a deep breath to calm her excitement. Despite the chilly air, the anticipation warmed her from within, a flicker of joy kindled by the simple act of recapturing a memory.

As she positioned herself for the shot, she carefully stepped closer to the water, her eyes focused on the spot where the waves met the shoreline. She stretched her arms out to mimic the pose in the old photograph. The cold wind nipped at her cheeks, but she was determined to recreate the essence of that moment - the happiness and innocence that seemed frozen in time.

However, as she shifted her weight onto her left foot, a sudden gust of wind blew her off balance. Her heart raced as she desperately tried to regain her footing, but it was too late. With a shout, Charlotte toppled into the freezing water, the icy chill momentarily stealing her breath away. She surfaced, sputtering and thrashing.

"Oi, would you look at that!" exclaimed one of the nearby fishermen, his laughter booming across the cove like a foghorn. His companions joined in, their hearty chuckles adding to the cacophony of crashing waves and squawking seagulls.

Mortified, Charlotte struggled with the weight of her soaked coat, shedding it in the water and managing to wade back to knee-high water before collapsing. She blinked the saltwater from her eyes, her cheeks flushed with embarrassment. She could feel the curious gazes of the fishermen on her, each laugh and smirk intensifying her mortification.

I can't believe I just did that.

Charlotte knew she had to get up and move on quickly, lest she wanted to become the laughingstock of Chesham Cove. Ignoring the sting of the icy water against her skin, she pushed herself up and waded back to shore, forcing a tight-lipped smile at the fishermen who continued to snicker at her expense.

"Quite the show, love," one of them called out, his words slurred by his accent. "Didn't know we 'ad ourselves a mermaid here!"

"Very funny," she called back through gritted teeth, wringing out her soaked sweater as she trudged back to where her phone lay, miraculously unharmed. Her coat was lost to the ocean. She picked her phone up, grateful for the small victory amid her current predicament, and tried to muster up the courage to face the fishermen again.

"Thank you for your concern," Charlotte said sarcastically, making sure to keep her voice steady despite the shivers that racked her body. "Now, if you'll excuse me, I have somewhere to be."

"Under the sea?" another fisherman hollered.

Charlotte turned away from the fishermen, attempting to salvage what little dignity she had left. As she walked away, slipping on the rocks at the water's edge, she noticed one of the fishermen had stopped laughing. He had a concerned expression on his face as he studied her closely, his eyes a warm shade of brown that stood out against the rugged features of his face. He was undeniably handsome, with the air of someone who'd spent a lifetime working outdoors.

"Are you alright?" he called out, genuine concern lacing his voice. Then, he strode toward her, his boots leaving deep imprints in the wet sand.

Charlotte hesitated for a moment, her pride warring with her need for help. "I'm fine," she finally replied, starting back up the shore and attempting a dismissive wave of her hand. But her voice wavered, and her legs trembled beneath her, betraying her true condition.

The man reached her side in an instant, his strong hand wrapping around her arm to steady her. The warmth of his touch seemed to seep into her cold, wet skin, providing a measure of comfort that she hadn't realized she needed.

"Easy now," he murmured, his grip firm yet gentle. "Let me help you up."

"Thank you," Charlotte said, allowing herself to lean on his sturdy frame. She could feel her cheeks burning with embarrassment, but there was something reassuring about his presence.

"Looks like the water got the best of you," the fisherman said lightly, his tone teasing but not unkind. "Happens to everyone at some point. Even mermaids. No need to be embarrassed."

Charlotte chuckled, despite her discomfort. "Well, I suppose there are worse ways to make a first impression," she admitted, feeling her spirits lift ever so slightly. "I could have half-drowned someone else."

"Indeed," Simon agreed, his laughter joining hers as they made their way back to the rocky shoreline. "And it's not every day I get to rescue a damsel in distress. Usually, it's just fish."

"Is that what I am?" Charlotte asked, her tone playful. "A damsel in distress?"

"Only for today," Simon replied with a wink, helping her onto a rock so she could sit and catch her breath. "But I have a feeling you're more than capable of handling yourself most days."

"Thank you," Charlotte said again, touched by his kindness. As she sat there, shivering and soaked to the bone, she felt a strange sense of gratitude.

The fisherman shrugged out of his thick corduroy coat and draped it around her as he raised a quizzical brow. "It's not often we find an American in Chesham Cove," he said, his voice carrying a hint of curiosity.

"Is it that obvious?" Charlotte asked with a sheepish grin. She'd always thought her New York accent to be subtle, but she supposed it must stand out in this small English town.

She clutched his coat around her and turned her nose into the collar. There was the unmistakable scent of fresh, outdoor air – she imagined his countless hours spent in the open, under the expansive sky. It was a crisp, invigorating smell, reminiscent of windswept fields and the faint trace of morning dew clinging to grass.

Underneath that was a subtle hint of woodsmoke, a smoky and slightly sweet fragrance. It spoke of evenings spent by the fire, crackling logs and stories shared and moments savored. This scent held the warmth of many nights, the comfort of flames that had warded off the coolness of the dusk.

Then there was the faintest whisper of motor oil, a rugged, earthy note that clung to the fibers. It was a hint that his hand were always busy fixing, tinkering, creating – the hands of a man who wasn't afraid to delve into work, to get his hands dirty, to solve problems.

Interesting.

"Let's just say you're a rare sight around these parts, Miss..." the man replied, his eyes sparkling with amusement. The wind tousled his hair, and the salty sea air filled Charlotte's nostrils, grounding her in the moment.

She almost said, *Moore,* but instead, she said, "Anderson. Charlotte Anderson. What brings you here, Mr..."

"Harris. But call me Simon. Born and raised here, actually. I'm a fisherman, if you couldn't tell," Simon explained, gesturing toward the group of fishermen nearby, who were still chuckling at the spectacle they had just witnessed.

"So are you here seeing family? You share a name with folks around these parts."

Charlotte furrowed her brow, thoughts racing. Could it be mere coincidence that there were others with her maiden name – Anderson – here in Chesham Cove? Was there a connection to her own family history that she was unaware of? This trip was supposed to be focused on her art and reconnecting with herself, but now, she found herself curious.

"No, just a pleasure trip. You travel ever?"

"A bit. But I couldn't imagine living anywhere else."

"Must be nice to be so connected to your roots," Charlotte murmured, feeling a slight pang of longing for her own tangled family history. She quickly shook off the thought, not wanting to let her introspection dampen the mood. With a deep breath, she stood up from the rock, her clothes dripping water onto the pebbles below.

"Thank you for your help, Simon," Charlotte said sincerely, meeting his gaze. She could feel her face flush under his steady stare, and she suddenly became very aware of her drenched state.

"Think nothing of it," Simon replied, his smile warm and genuine. "Just glad I could lend a hand."

"Still, I appreciate it," Charlotte insisted, then, unable to quell her rising blush, added, "I should probably get to The Crown Inn and change into something dry."

"Of course," Simon agreed, nodding toward the path that led away from the cove. "Keep the coat. I'll get it back when I see you next. Take care of yourself, Charlotte."

She offered him a small smile before turning on her heel, her wet shoes squelching with each step. As she walked away, Charlotte replayed the encounter in her mind, feeling both mortification and curiosity.

When I see you next.

As she reclaimed her suitcase from the sidewalk and walked, her thoughts drifted back to Simon – his rugged features, strong yet gentle hands, and the way he had rushed to her aid. There was something about Simon that intrigued her, lingering like a soft melody at the edge of her consciousness—but for now, she needed to focus on warming up and getting dry. There would be time to explore Chesham Cove and the secrets of its residents later.

The Crown Inn beckoned, promising a sanctuary from the cold. Perhaps tomorrow, she would look for answers about the Anderson family connection that Simon had alluded to.

"All right," she whispered to herself. "Time to see what The Crown Inn has in store for me."

CHAPTER ELEVEN

The building had seen better days.

The Crown Inn stood in front of her, a behemoth. Its paint was chipped and faded, woodwork warped by time and the salty sea air. Yet, despite its run-down appearance, there was an undeniable charm to it that drew Charlotte in. As an artist, Charlotte could see the stories hidden within every crack and crevice.

Stepping up to the porch, she stretched her weary limbs, taking a deep breath of the crisp ocean air. Her eyes wandered to the horizon, where the sun was dipping low toward the water's edge, casting a symphony of warm hues across the sky. The breathtaking view of the ocean from the inn felt like a soothing balm to her soul, which had been wound tight for far too long. As Charlotte gazed at the melding colors of the sunset, she allowed herself to be swept up in the tranquility of the moment. It was as if the weight of the world had been momentarily lifted from her shoulders, replaced by the gentle caress of the wind and the rhythmic lull of the waves crashing against the shore. This place held promises of serenity, if she were willing to open her heart to it.

Charlotte withdrew her gaze from the mesmerizing horizon and turned toward the inn's entrance when she heard the creak of the weathered wooden door. A woman with a kind smile appeared, her face lined with the wisdom of time, her silver hair pinned up neatly. Her eyes held a gentle warmth that seemed to mirror the soul—if not the age—of the inn itself.

"Ah! You must be Charlotte!" the woman exclaimed, extending a hand gnarled by years of hard work. "I'm Margaret Wright, owner of The Crown Inn. But please, call me Marge."

"Nice to meet you, Marge," Charlotte replied as she shook the woman's hand, sensing the stories behind each wrinkle.

"Welcome, my dear. I'm so sorry to tell you, but..." Marge studied her for a moment and then chuckled softly. "My grandson set up this online booking thing, you see. I don't know much about it, but he insisted it was the way to go. I only just saw that you were coming an hour ago on the computer."

Charlotte smiled at Marge's confession, feeling a kinship with the woman who seemed so grounded in tradition amidst the ever-changing world. She admired the determination it must have taken for Marge to maintain her beloved inn while adapting to modernity—or at least being dragged toward it by a grandchild.

"Your grandson sounds like a smart young man," Charlotte said sincerely, and Marge beamed with pride.

"Indeed, he is," Marge agreed, her voice laced with affection. "But enough about me and my ignorance of technology. You look soaked! Chilled to the bone. Let's get you settled in, shall we?"

"Oh, yes," Charlotte replied, her teeth chattering from the cold. "It's lovely to meet you. I'm afraid I had a bit of an accident near the cove. I fell into the water."

"Goodness, dear! Come inside and warm yourself by the fire. We'll get you a hot cup of tea and you can get some dry clothes," the woman said, ushering her inside. "Musn't have you expiring on the lawn, you being my first online customer and all."

"Thank you, Marge. I'm honored," Charlotte replied with a grin, stepping into the warm, darkened confines of the inn. The scent of aged wood and a hint of lavender filled her nostrils, immediately enveloping her in a sense of comfort.

"Right this way, love." Marge led Charlotte down a narrow hallway adorned with faded paintings of seascapes and portraits of long-gone residents. The worn wooden floorboards creaked beneath their feet, each step echoing like whispers of the past.

As they reached the foot of an imposing staircase, Marge gestured upward with a weathered hand. "Our rooms are upstairs, dear. I do hope you don't mind a bit of a climb."

Charlotte glanced at the winding stairs, noting the intricate carvings on the banister and the tattered edges of the carpet runner. She found herself captivated by the unique blend of craftsmanship and wear that seemed to embody the essence of the inn itself. "Not at all," she reassured Marge. "It's beautiful."

"Ah, thank you." Marge's voice softened with pride as they began their ascent. Charlotte tried not to let her suitcase wheels bump the stairs. "My great-grandfather built this place, you know. His hands crafted these very stairs."

Charlotte's fingers traced the grooves of the delicate carvings as they climbed, feeling the history of the place seep into her skin. The inn was a living demonstration of the love and dedication of generations, and she was deeply moved by it. As they neared the top, she paused to catch her breath, looking back down at the ornate entrance below.

"Quite a view, isn't it?" Marge commented, following her gaze. "I've always loved this staircase. There's something about it that makes you feel like you're ascending into another world."

Charlotte agreed. The inn seemed to be a portal to a simpler time, a refuge from the chaos of her life outside its walls. She inhaled deeply, taking in the musty scent of old books and the faintest hint of sea air.

"Let me show you to your room," Marge said, breaking the silence. As they continued up the stairs, Charlotte felt a strange sense of anticipation, as though she were on the verge of discovering something wonderful.

And perhaps, she thought, she truly was.

Marge pushed open the door, revealing a room that made it feel as though Charlotte had stepped back in time, entering a space where the ghosts of the past still lingered. The rustic atmosphere brought to mind images of another era—it was both fascinating and a little creepy.

"Here we are," Marge said, her voice softening as she gestured for Charlotte to enter.

Charlotte stepped inside, her eyes darting between the worn wooden furniture and the faded wallpaper that adorned the walls. She felt drawn to the room's enigmatic aura while simultaneously feeling a chill run down her spine.

"Is everything to your liking?" Marge inquired, her gaze steady on Charlotte.

"It's... intriguing," Charlotte replied, not quite able to put into words the emotions swirling within her. "It's like stepping into another world."

"Ah, yes," Marge nodded, a knowing smile gracing her lips. "This inn has a way of transporting you, doesn't it?"

As Charlotte moved further into the room, she traced her fingers along the rough surface of an antique dresser, feeling the history etched into every groove. Her heart raced as she took in the creaky floorboards and the cobwebs that clung to the corners, wondering what secrets the room held. And what insects.

"Many guests have come and gone over the years," Marge said, her voice taking on a wistful tone. "Some say they've felt the presence of those who walked these halls long before us."

"Do you believe in those things?" Charlotte asked, her voice hushed as if speaking louder might disturb the spirits.

"Who am I to say?" Marge shrugged, her eyes twinkling with mischief. "Perhaps some things are better left unknown."

A shiver coursed through Charlotte's body as she considered the possibility, her curiosity piqued by the enigma that surrounded her.

"Thank you for showing me the room, Marge," Charlotte said, turning her gaze back to the older woman. "It's certainly a place I won't soon forget."

"Of course, dear," Marge replied warmly. "Shall I light the fire?" She gestured to the fireplace, which had been laid with an unlit stack of wood.

"I'll manage," Charlotte said, just wanting to be alone so that she could decompress.

With that, Marge tutted and fussed with the curtains and bedspread before she closed the door behind her, leaving Charlotte alone with her thoughts and the whispers of the past that had clearly once screamed through these halls. Charlotte touched off the fire with one of the long matches she found in a metal case on the mantel. Soon, the dry logs roared with flame, and she turned to peel out of Simon's coat, hanging it on a cast iron hook that was to the left of the fireplace.

Her clothes were next, exchanged for a dry pair of flannel sleep pants and a grey t-shirt to match the skies outside. If she went out, she could use the hoodie she had packed. She'd get a new coat tomorrow. But lethargy stole over her, and she doubted she'd be venturing back out tonight.

As Charlotte stood there, by the fire, her eyes roving over the room's rustic charm, she was drawn to a window obscured by heavy curtains. With a gentle tug, she pulled them aside and opened the window, revealing a breathtaking view of the ocean beyond. The vast expanse of water stretched out endlessly, its surface shimmering beneath the setting sun like a canvas splattered with molten gold. The horizon seemed to merge with the sky.

Leaning against the windowsill, she allowed herself a moment of quiet reflection. She thought of Daniel and how he would never have encouraged her to take this trip. It had been years since she had felt truly alive, but now, as her eyes drank in the stunning vista, she could feel the stirrings of something new awakening within her.

Charlotte settled into a rocking chair by the fireplace, and the warmth enveloped her. She found herself beginning to relax. Her thoughts turned to the stories Marge had shared with her earlier. If the walls of this inn were indeed haunted by the spirits of the past, perhaps

51

they could also serve as muses. Hopefully, none of them would object to a visiting American—not like the cheeky fishermen by the shore earlier.

A gentle knock on the door pulled Charlotte from her reverie, and she turned to find Marge standing in the doorway, looking tentative. She held a small tray laden with a teapot, a steaming cup, and a plate of homemade scones and jam.

"Thought you might appreciate a little something to warm you up," Marge offered, setting the tray down on a nearby table. "It can get quite chilly here by the water, especially at night."

"Thank you, Marge," Charlotte replied, her heart swelling with gratitude. "This is so kind of you."

"Also, there's plenty of firewood stacked in the next room if you'd like to build up your fire later tonight," Marge added. "My grandson laid this one you have now, good fella. I can't haul the logs myself— bad shoulder, you know—but there's nothing quite like the crackle of a fire to make a place feel truly cozy."

"That sounds wonderful," Charlotte agreed, already envisioning herself curled up in front of the flames, a sketchbook resting on her lap as she dozed off. "I'll definitely go grab some extra if I need it."

"Good." Marge smiled, her face crinkling like well-worn parchment. "And if you need anything else – anything at all – don't hesitate to ask. I'm just a holler away."

"Thank you, Marge," Charlotte repeated, feeling a knot of tension in her chest begin to loosen. "Your hospitality has been truly exceptional."

"Think nothing of it, dear," Marge assured her, patting her hand gently. "You're our *first* online guest, after all. We ought to make sure you have a memorable stay. Winston says we should be sure the yaps are good for afterwards."

Charlotte grinned. "Yelps?"

"Could be," Marge said. "Don't depend on my memory."

Charlotte took a sip of the tea, savoring the warmth that spread through her body, chasing away the chill that clung to her bones. She glanced around the room, her eyes lingering on the creaking floorboards and the faded wallpaper that told a tale of years gone by.

"Actually," she said as she looked back at Marge, "I was wondering if you could tell me more about the history of the inn."

"Ah," Marge's eyes twinkled with mischief, a knowing smile playing at the corner of her lips as she shuffled toward the door. "Well, there's certainly no shortage of stories to be found here. But my bones are tired, and I'm sure yours are, too. Maybe tomorrow."

Charlotte felt a pang of disappointment—but she nodded in agreement.

"Until then, enjoy your tea and biscuits," Marge said, giving Charlotte one last reassuring smile before she turned to leave. "And remember, I'm always here if you need me."

Charlotte watched as Marge disappeared out the door and down the winding staircase, her footsteps echoing through the dimly lit halls. Marge might be soon joining dreamland, but Charlotte knew that sleep would be elusive tonight – her mind was too alive with anxious thoughts – but she also understood that rest was essential if she wished to fully explore the possibility she was seeking here in England.

She made short work of the warm scones with cherry jam, and then set her tea cup aside and stood. Despite her doubts about sleep, she climbed into the four-poster bed, grabbing her phone to text Amelia, and then, Roxanne. Then, Charlotte laid down in the downy, slightly flowery bed linens. Her eyelids drooped. Maybe she would run into a posh, refined English ghost or two in her dreams—and hopefully avoid any *personal* ghosts of her own that might have followed her to Chesham.

CHAPTER TWELVE

Charlotte's hand lingered on the doorknob as she stepped out of her room the next morning, taking a moment to absorb her surroundings. The worn wooden floors of The Crown Inn creaked gently beneath her feet, echoing the whispers of countless guests who had walked these halls before her. She wondered, amusedly, how they had booked before young Winston had put his grandmother online.

She inhaled deeply, the comforting smell of old books and aged wood filling her senses. As an artist, Charlotte appreciated the beauty of things that had lived a life, their stories etched into their very essence. She could see the history embedded in every groove and knot of the floorboards, the walls, the ceilings, and she felt a sense of connection to the place – a connection that reached beyond just a temporary stop would warrant.

"Ah, there you are!" Marge, the innkeeper, greeted her with a warm smile from across the hall. "I hope you slept well."

"Like a baby," Charlotte replied, returning the smile. "I didn't think I would, but I dropped right off."

Marge chuckled, her eyes twinkling with pride. "No ghosts, then?"

"None to be seen. I'm a little disappointed." Charlotte's gaze wandered down the hallway, curious to explore the rest of the inn. "Would you mind if I had a look around?"

"Of course not! Feel free to wander wherever your heart desires," Marge said with a welcoming wave of her hand.

"Thank you." Charlotte set off, her footsteps muffled by the plush carpet that lined the ground floor. Each room she entered revealed a new glimpse into the inn's past, as though she were peeling back layers of time.

In the parlor, she ran her fingers over velvety armchairs arranged around a grand fireplace, imagining generations of travelers warming themselves by the fire after long journeys. A polished oak table stood proudly in the center of the room, its surface adorned with intricate carvings that spoke of skilled hands and hours of painstaking labor.

Through a set of elegant double doors, she found herself in a library that seemed to defy the laws of space, filled to the brim with books on every subject imaginable, and then some.

"Isn't it wonderful?" Marge had appeared quietly behind her, careful not to startle her guest. "I've spent years collecting these books. Some came down through the family, some I found in dusty old shops, others were gifts from my guests."

Charlotte's fingers traced the spines of several volumes. "It's incredible," she agreed.

Charlotte's fingers lingered on the last book on the shelf before she tore herself away from the library. The artist in her yearned to explore every corner of this enchanting inn, to unravel all the stories that whispered through its timeworn walls. She stepped back into the hallway and found herself facing a second, winding staircase that led upwards. With a deep, steadying breath, she began to climb.

The banister felt smooth beneath her fingertips, its intricate carvings telling their own tales of craftsmanship and years of use. Charlotte marveled at the details, her mind creating images of those who had slid their hands along these same curves long ago. Maybe a duke, or a baron—a handsome one.

Maybe a fisherman. A handsome one, she thought, thinking of the coat hanging, now dry, in her room, unneeded now that she had a new coat of her own.

The steps creaked softly under her feet, each one imbued with the echoes of countless guests who had ascended before her.

Marge called from below. "Don't forget to take a peek at the balcony when you reach the third floor."

"Of course, thank you," Charlotte replied, glancing down at her host with a smile. She continued her ascent, her curiosity piqued by Marge's suggestion.

As she reached the third floor, Charlotte discovered the small balcony hidden between two guest rooms. Stepping out onto it, she was immediately struck by the quiet beauty of the courtyard below. Green ivy crawled up the stone walls, intertwining with delicate blossoms that swayed gently in the breeze. The rain from yesterday had cleared, and she could hear birdsong and the distant lapping of waves, a symphony that spoke to her heart.

"Imagine the potential," she murmured, picturing guests enjoying their morning coffee or stealing a quiet moment of reflection in this serene oasis. "This place is truly magical."

Feeling the solid oak of the banister under her fingers again, Charlotte continued up the stairs to the fourth floor. The air grew warmer as she ascended higher into the heart of this grand building. Charlotte pushed open a door that revealed a cozy attic space with slanted ceilings and a window that offered a glimpse of the nearby coastline. Sunlight streamed in through the dusty panes, casting dappled patterns on the wooden floorboards below.

This would be an absolutely perfect studio. She imagined herself sitting by the window, paintbrush in hand, immortalizing the beauty of the sea on canvas. Or perhaps, curled up in a plush armchair with a good book, letting the salty breeze whisk her away to far-off lands.

Descending the worn staircase, Charlotte's thoughts lingered on the attic space as she reached the ground floor. She took a moment to appreciate the warm glow of the morning sun filtering through the antique windows before making her way toward the basement door. The musty scent of old wood and damp earth clung to the air as she opened it, revealing a narrow stone staircase that led downward into the underbelly of the inn.

Charlotte ducked beneath an exposed beam as she entered the basement. The coolness of the subterranean space sent a shiver down her spine. She quickly turned back, making a mental note to save the basement exploration for another day. Maybe Marge's ghost stories really were getting to her.

As she climbed back up the creaking wooden staircase, to distract her spooked mind, Charlotte envisioned the transformation that might be possible at The Crown Inn. Her artist's eye saw potential in every corner, her mind brimming with ideas for how to breathe new life into this storied building— opening up the ground floor, cozy reading nooks on the third floor, every floor something unique. It would be a huge undertaking, and she couldn't imagine the money it would take, but the thought of a restored Crown Inn lingered in the back of her mind.

"Marge," she called out, finding the innkeeper polishing a brass candlestick at the front desk. "The inn is wonderful, it's got so much character. And that attic space is just begging to be turned into an artist's haven." Charlotte leaned against the desk, her gaze drifting towards the entrance. "I was thinking of grabbing some breakfast at The Laughing Lobster."

"Oh, you'll love it there," Marge enthused, setting down the candlestick. "Best seafood omelet in town, and their blueberry pancakes are to die for. Tell them Marge sent you, and they might just slip you an extra treat."

Laughing, Charlotte nodded. "I'll be sure to do that. Thanks for everything, Marge. This place... it's really something."

Marge's eyes twinkled with a hint of mischief. "You just wait. It's even more enchanting when the full moon rises. Makes you believe in magic, it does."

Charlotte shouldered her bag. "I'll be back later. Who knows, maybe I'll get some inspiration for a painting while I'm out."

As she stepped out of the inn, the crisp morning air greeted her, carrying the scent of the sea. She turned to wave goodbye to Marge.

With a spring in her step, Charlotte headed towards The Laughing Lobster, her heart light. She realized, as she walked, that she hadn't thought of Daniel all morning.

CHAPTER THIRTEEN

Charlotte pushed open the heavy wooden door of the pub, warmth and laughter cascading out into the cool morning air. She stepped inside, the smell of bacon mingling with the sound of lively chatter that filled the room. A fire crackled in the hearth, casting a soft glow on the rustic wooden tables and cozy nooks that seemed to invite patrons to stay awhile.

"Ah, there she is!" a voice called from behind her, and Charlotte turned to see the fishermen from earlier entering the pub. Their clothes were still damp from what must have been their dawn trolling, but their spirits seemed far from dampened.

"Look, everyone, it's the Soggy Yank!" one of them proclaimed, eliciting chuckles from the group.

Charlotte smiled thinly. "Alright, alright," she said, rolling her eyes. "I suppose I'll take that nickname for now. But only because one of you lot was so nice to me afterward."

The fishermen laughed, clapping each other on the back as they made their way toward their usual table in the corner. She found a quaint spot near the window, where the golden rays of the sun cast a delicate glow on the wooden surface. She pulled out the chair and took a seat, a small sigh escaping her lips.

"Charlotte, right?" a deep voice asked from behind her.

She looked up to find Simon Harris standing there, his hands tucked into the pockets of his worn jeans. His rugged appearance was softened by the warmth in his eyes, and in the light from the window, the brown of them was flecked with gold. She felt butterflies start up in her stomach.

"Simon," she replied, her voice carrying a hint of surprise. "Fancy meeting you here."

"Mind if I join you?" he asked, gesturing to the empty chair across from hers.

Her heart fluttered momentarily. She was caught off guard by the prospect of spending the meal with him. She hesitated, wondering what Daniel would think if he were to see them together.

He gave up that right, she thought.

"Of course. Please, have a seat," she said, offering a warm smile.

"Thank you," Simon replied, pulling out the chair and settling down across from her. His presence seemed to fill the space between them, creating an energy that both intrigued and intimidated her.

As they exchanged pleasantries, Charlotte noticed how the same light from outside danced playfully across Simon's weathered features, highlighting the lines and contours of his face. She found herself drawn to his warm, earthy scent, which reminded her of damp soil after a rainfall - a far cry from the sterile, manufactured cologne that always clung to Daniel.

"Quite a day already today," Simon said, breaking her reverie. "We took in twice what we expected."

"Oh?" she replied, her gaze momentarily shifting toward the fishermen in the corner. She pursed her lips at the nickname, *Soggy Yank*. But if not for that embarrassing incident, would she have talked with Simon at the water's edge? "Any mermaids?"

He laughed, and it was as deep and hearty as the waves crashing against the craggy shore. "You're the first, and I suspect the only, Charlotte," he responded, a sincere smile lighting up his face.

Then, his phone rang. He gave her an apologetic smile and looked at the screen. Then, he winced.

"Cripes. It's work. I'm so sorry, I have to go."

"Oh! That's okay. Duty calls." She felt a pang of disappointment—but she tried not to show it.

He pulled out his wallet and put down several bills. "Listen, breakfast is on me. But only if you'll meet me back here at half past seven tonight."

"I'll be there," she replied, feeling a surge of excitement. It was just the sort of thing she needed—and who knew, maybe he was a duke in disguise? Regardless, the man across from her was certainly interesting enough to have an evening drink with.

Simon stood, his chair scraping gently against the floor. " I'm really looking forward to it."

"Me too," Charlotte said, her heart fluttering slightly. "Thanks for the invitation, Simon."

As Simon left, Charlotte watched him through the window, making his way back to the harbor. She felt a giddy sense of anticipation.

"Yank, are you sweet on Simon?" one of the fishermen called from the corner, and the rest of them began making kissing noises in the air.

Charlotte turned and narrowed her eyes at them. "I'm sweet on any man I can drag down into the sea, boys." Then, she bared her teeth, and they dissolved into a raucous bout of laughter, toasting her with their coffee cups.

That evening, after a long, luxuriously lazy day spent in her room sketching, Charlotte approached The Laughing Lobster, her heart skipping a beat with a mixture of nervous excitement and anticipation. As she entered the pub, she scanned the room, and her eyes landed on Simon, who was waiting for her at the bar.

He spotted her and waved, a bright smile lighting up his face. Dressed casually in a button-down shirt and jeans, he exuded a relaxed confidence. "Charlotte, over here!" he called out.

She made her way over, feeling a flutter of excitement in her stomach. "Hi, Simon," she greeted him, taking the seat beside him at the bar. "This place is even livelier than it was this morning."

"It's a popular spot," Simon chuckled. "Well, it's the only spot in town. Great for unwinding after a long day."

The bartender approached, and they ordered drinks – a glass of red wine for Charlotte and a local ale for Simon. As they waited for their drinks, Simon turned to her with a curious glint in his eyes.

"So, tell me more about what brought you to The Crown Inn," he said, leaning slightly closer. "Marge has been all too secretive about the new girl in town."

Charlotte laughed, sipping her wine. "Well, there's not much to tell yet. I'm still figuring things out. I guess you could say I'm on an artist's retreat."

Their conversation flowed effortlessly from there, touching on topics from their favorite books—inspired by Charlotte's description of Marge's library—and travel experiences to the quirky histories of the town's landmarks. Simon's knowledge of literature and his love for the town were evident in every word he spoke, and Charlotte found herself completely engrossed.

As the evening wore on, the pub's crowd thinned out, leaving a more intimate setting. The bartender began to dim the lights, casting a cozy glow over the remaining patrons.

"You know," Simon said, his voice low and warm, "I have a feeling you're going to fit right in here."

Charlotte felt a warmth spread through her at his words. There was something comforting about Simon's presence, something that made her feel like she was exactly where she was meant to be. And although Charlotte's heart still ached for Daniel, she couldn't deny that Simon's presence had ignited a spark within her - one she hadn't felt in years.

"I hope so," she replied, her smile reflecting the optimism that cautiously bubbled inside her. "Chesham Cove is a beautiful place. I can see why people are drawn to it."

Simon chuckled. "Yes, it has a certain charm to it. The weather can be a bit temperamental, though."

"Kind of like an artist's temperament?" she asked with a playful grin.

"Exactly," he agreed, his laughter mingling with hers.

When the bartender approached their table to take their next drink orders, Simon ordered an English bitters

"English bitters?" Charlotte echoed, curiosity evident in her tone. "I've never had one before. Truth be told, I don't know much about beer."

"Really?" Simon raised an eyebrow, intrigued. "Well, if you're interested, I could give you a little lesson in British beers."

"Maybe another time," she demurred, feeling slightly out of her depth when it came to the world of ales and lagers. For now, she was content to stick with what she knew. Good old red wine.

"Fair enough," Simon conceded, taking a sip of his beer when it arrived. "But you really should try this just once. It's a quintessential British experience."

Charlotte hesitated, her fingers drumming lightly against the stem of her wine glass. She glanced down at her own drink, then back up at Simon's inviting gaze. There was something about Simon, with his rugged charm and easygoing nature, that made her want to step out of her comfort zone.

"Alright," she finally acquiesced, reaching for the glass of bitters. "Here goes nothing."

"Cheers," Simon responded with a grin, watching as Charlotte lifted the glass to her lips. His eyes twinkled, anticipating her reaction to the unfamiliar taste.

The moment the liquid touched her tongue, Charlotte's face scrunched up involuntarily in distaste, a shudder rippling through her body. Her hand instinctively pulled away from her mouth, leaving the glass hovering uncertainly in midair. Simon caught the glass and returned it to the table. The bitterness had been so much more potent than she'd expected, catching her off guard.

"Wow," she managed, her voice wavering slightly as she tried to regain her composure. "That's... that's quite something."

"Too strong for your taste?" Simon asked, struggling to suppress a chuckle.

"Maybe just a little," Charlotte admitted, her cheeks flushed with both embarrassment and amusement. She took a steadying sip of her wine to wash away the lingering bitterness.

"Ah well," Simon said, his eyes crinkling at the corners with genuine warmth. "I suppose it's not for everyone. But I'm glad you gave it a go – that's what life's all about, isn't it? Trying new things, even if they don't always turn out as planned."

Charlotte smiled in return. As she looked into Simon's understanding eyes, it was exactly what she needed in this moment – someone who could challenge her to take risks, but also be there to catch her when she fell. She realized, with a jolt, that she had never felt that with Daniel. She had always felt that she was the one who had to be there to offer the soft place to land, and he had been out in the world, taking all the risks—only to pull away from her for staying in the place he'd put her.

Still grinning, Charlotte turned her attention to the menu. "I think I'll stick to what I know," she decided, flagging down the passing bartender. "Could I please have one last glass of your house red?"

"Of course, miss," he said, giving her a polite nod before disappearing back into the throng of patrons. Even though he seemed a bit harried, Charlotte appreciated his friendly smile and attentive service.

Soon enough, the bartender returned with her glass of red wine. It wasn't the most exceptional wine she'd ever had, but it felt comforting, like an old friend.

"Much better," she sighed, looking up at Simon with a contented smile. "And much more familiar."

Simon raised his glass in a toast. "To finding comfort in the familiar, even when we're far from home," he said, his eyes warm and inviting.

The sound of boisterous laughter drew their attention to the group of fishermen from earlier. They were huddled together at their same table, casting conspiratorial glances toward Charlotte and Simon. One of them, a burly man with a bushy beard, raised his glass and whistled, calling out good-naturedly, "Oi, Simon! Looks like you've caught yourself a fine catch there!"

"Do you take them with you everywhere you go?" she asked dryly.

"They follow me around like dogs," he returned, his expression apologetic.

"Ah. My next guess was that they simply all live here, at The Laughing Lobster."

Simon chuckled, shaking his head at the playful teasing, while Charlotte felt her cheeks warm. She watched as Simon ran a hand through his tousled hair, a sheepish grin playing on his lips.

"Pay them no mind, Charlotte," he reassured her. "They're a harmless lot, really, just always looking for a bit of fun. They're good men."

"Seems like they enjoy giving you a hard time," Charlotte observed, sipping her wine with a smirk.

"It comes with the territory," Simon admitted, his gaze momentarily flicking to the fishermen before returning to Charlotte. "We work hard together, but we also play hard. It's how we keep our spirits up."

"Back home, I never really had anything like that," Charlotte confessed, her voice tinged with wistfulness. "A close-knit group of friends who could always count on one another. I had—have—my sister, but that's about it."

"Maybe that's something you can find here," Simon suggested softly, his eyes searching hers for a moment before he looked away.

A mischievous glint flashed in Charlotte's eyes as she caught Simon's gaze. "Well then, maybe it's time I joined in on the fun," she declared, her voice resolute.

"Really?" Simon asked, his eyebrows raised in surprise. "What do you have in mind?"

"Watch and learn," she replied cryptically, setting down her wine glass with a determined clink. Charlotte turned her attention to the fishermen, who were still chuckling amongst themselves. With a deep breath, she called out, "Oi! You lot over there!"

The boisterous table fell silent, their eyes drawn to Charlotte like magnets. She could feel her heart pounding in her chest but pushed aside her nerves, focusing instead on the twinkle of challenge in the fishermen's eyes.

"Seems to me you've been having quite a laugh at our expense tonight," she began, her tone light yet pointed. "But I can't help but wonder... How well can you all take a joke yourselves?"

"Oho!" one of the men hooted, leaning back in his chair and thumping his fist on the table. "The Soggy Yank's got some fire in her, eh?"

"Indeed, she does," Charlotte retorted, fighting to suppress a grin as she locked eyes with the fisherman. "So, tell me, which one of you fine gentlemen is responsible for reeling in the smallest catch today?"

A chorus of laughter erupted from the group, along with some good-natured finger-pointing and denials. One man, his face red as a beet, finally conceded defeat amidst the jeering of his friends.

"Ah, there we have it," Charlotte said, giving him a playful nod. "Well, sir, this Soggy Yank wants to remind you that, where I'm from, that means that you are the one to buy the next round for everyone at your table."

"Or what?" he clipped back.

"Mermaid's curse. You risk bad luck in the next catch."

He narrowed his eyes at her, then grinned. "Fair enough, Soggy Yank," the fisherman replied, raising his pint glass in her direction.

"Cheers!" Charlotte called out, lifting her own glass as the table of fishermen erupted into laughter and applause.

As the fishermen carried on with their good-natured ribbing, now of their compatriot instead of her and Simon, Simon leaned in closer to Charlotte, his eyes sparkling with amusement. "I'm rather impressed. You certainly held your own against them."

"Thank you," she replied, her cheeks flushed with excitement. "It was... invigorating, actually."

"A bit of courage, and you're a whole different woman," Simon murmured, his gaze lingering on her face for a moment longer before he took another sip of his beer.

And as the laughter continued to fill the pub, Charlotte found herself wondering if the same could be true for matters of the heart, as well.

And, as she sipped her wine and took a sidelong glance at Simon, she thought, *I might just try it.*

CHAPTER FOURTEEN

The soft glow of the pub's remaining candles flickered, dancing shadows across Charlotte and Simon's faces as they sat opposite one another, now at a table. A once bustling room had quieted, leaving them with nothing but the hum of their conversation to fill the space.

"Did you always know you wanted to be an artist?" Simon asked, his eyes bright with genuine interest.

"Ever since I was a little girl," Charlotte replied, her voice tinged with nostalgia. "I remember spending hours drawing pictures in my sketchbook and dreaming of having my own gallery someday."

"And you've made that dream come true, haven't you?"

"No. I was rejected from a gallery right before I went home to find Daniel packing." She winced and hesitated for a moment before continuing. "But I have always found solace in art, especially during difficult times."

Simon nodded, understanding the unspoken emotions behind her words. He took a sip of his beer, savoring the bitterness on his tongue before he spoke again. "So, what really brought you to Chesham Cove, Charlotte? It's not exactly a bustling art scene. Is it the distance? Not like your lad's going to come across the pond to get you to sign divorce papers."

Charlotte looked down at her hands, the worn wooden table providing a backdrop for her thoughts. "I guess I just needed a change," she said slowly, choosing her words carefully. "After everything with Daniel, I wanted to feel connected to something again. To find a place where I could heal and rediscover who I am. There was this old picture of me, my dad, Roxanne. We came here once when I was twelve. I guess I'm just reaching."

"Chesham Cove has a way of doing that," Simon agreed, his voice gentle. "There's something about this place that makes you feel grounded."

"Yeah, I feel it," Charlotte whispered, her heart swelling at the realization that someone understood her desire for connection.

Simon glanced around the near-empty pub, his gaze settling back on Charlotte. "You know, you mentioned earlier that your maiden name was Anderson," he said thoughtfully. "There's a few families with that name in this area. Maybe you have some long-lost relatives here in Chesham Cove? It could be worth looking into if you're searching for a connection."

Charlotte raised her eyebrows in surprise, considering the possibility. "I never really thought about that," she admitted. "But you might be right. It could be interesting to learn more about my family history." A soft smile touched her lips as she imagined uncovering her roots in this quaint seaside village.

The pub owner approached their table, a friendly smile on his face. "Evening, folks," he said kindly, handing the bill to Simon. "I'm afraid it's time for me to close up shop for the night. I hope you two enjoyed yourselves."

"Thank you," Charlotte replied, smiling at the older man. "We had a lovely evening."

Simon nodded in agreement, unearthing some money and paying, despite Charlotte's protests, and then sliding off his stool and offering a hand to Charlotte. She took it gratefully, feeling a jolt of electricity run through her as their fingers intertwined. Together, they walked out of the pub, leaving the warm interior behind and stepping into the cool night air.

The moon cast a gentle light over the cobblestone streets as they strolled toward the inn, its silvery beams glinting off the waves crashing against the shore. The salty sea breeze brushed against Charlotte's cheeks, filling her lungs with each breath she took.

"Isn't it beautiful out here?" Charlotte asked. "There's something so soothing about the sea at night."

Simon nodded, his eyes sparkling with the reflection of the moonlight on the water. "It is," he agreed.

As they approached the inn, the warm glow from its windows seemed to beckon them closer. Charlotte's heart raced with anticipation, unsure of what the end of the evening would bring. The cobblestone path beneath her feet felt solid and real, grounding her amid the whirlwind of emotions swirling within.

"Thank you for tonight, Simon," she said, her voice soft and sincere. "I haven't enjoyed myself like this in a long time."

Simon flashed her a warm smile, the creases around his eyes deepening as he did so. "The pleasure was all mine, Charlotte. It's been wonderful getting to know you."

They stopped just outside the inn's entrance, the sound of the waves still present but distant, like a heartbeat thrumming in the background. Charlotte could feel the warmth radiating from Simon's body, his closeness both thrilling and terrifying her in equal measure.

"Goodnight, Charlotte," Simon murmured, his voice carrying the faintest hint of reluctance.

"Goodnight," she whispered back, her breath hitching in her throat as she gathered her courage. In that moment, she decided to take a chance, leaning in to kiss him. The faint scent of sea salt hung in the air as Charlotte leaned in, her lips drawing closer to Simon's. The moment seemed suspended in time, as if the universe held its breath, waiting. Her heart pounded wildly, awaiting his reaction.

But as their lips were about to meet, Simon gently ducked away, his eyes wide with surprise. "Charlotte," he stammered, his rugged hands coming up to lightly touch her shoulders, "I'm... I'm sorry, but I don't kiss on the first date."

A wave of embarrassment washed over Charlotte, tinting her cheeks a deep shade of pink. She felt immediately foolish for misreading the situation. "I –" she hesitated, trying to find the right words. "I'm *so* sorry, Simon. I thought... well, I don't know what I thought."

Simon's fingers gave her shoulders a reassuring squeeze before dropping back to his sides. "No need to apologize," he said gently, his gaze warm and understanding. "It's just a personal rule of mine. It doesn't mean I didn't enjoy our time together or that I'm not interested in seeing you again."

Charlotte bit her lip, her mind racing. She wished she could turn back time and undo her impulsive gesture.

"Really, Charlotte," Simon said gently. "I enjoyed our time together tonight. I'd like to get to know you better." His words rang sincere, and his gaze held hers, offering a lifeline amidst her embarrassment.

Relief washed over her like the tide. She looked down at the cobblestones beneath their feet, gathering her thoughts. "I'm sorry if I misinterpreted the moment. It's just... I haven't felt this connected to someone in such a long time."

"You didn't do anything wrong," he told her, his voice warm and comforting. "These things happen. I mean, I've never had a mermaid try to French me on a first date, but maybe you American mermaids do things differently."

She laughed. It released the tension between them.

"Let's take it one step at a time, shall we?" Simon suggested, his hand rising again, thumb tracing small circles on her shoulder, anchoring her further.

Charlotte nodded, finally meeting his gaze once again. "Yes, let's do that. One step at a time," she agreed, her voice regaining strength.

"Goodnight, Charlotte," Simon murmured, releasing her shoulder and stepping back.

"Goodnight, Simon," she replied, watching as he turned and walked away, his broad silhouette melding with the shadows.

As Charlotte entered the inn, she clung to the seeds of hope that had taken root, unsure if they might nurture them into something beautiful and lasting, or if Simon might just turn out to be a nice memory one day, like the picture. For now, one step at a time would be enough.

Once inside her cozy room, Charlotte closed the door behind her and leaned against it, her heart still racing from the events of the evening. She could still feel the cool night air on her cheeks and the faint echo of Simon's laughter in her ears from their time at The Lobster. Images from their conversation at the pub danced through her mind – the way Simon's face had lit up when talking about his fishing adventures and how they had shared stories of their childhoods.

And, of course, she couldn't help but cringe as she remembered leaning in for the kiss, her eyes closing in anticipation only to be met with Simon's evasion. "I can't believe I did that," she muttered, shaking her head.

Thoughts of Daniel suddenly weighed heavily on her heart, and guilt tangled itself around her like the ivy on The Crown.

"He's barely left me, and I'm trying to kiss another man," she scolded herself, shaking her head as if it could dispel the unease that clung to her. She paced the small space of her room. The floorboards creaked beneath her feet, echoing her inner turmoil.

When she finally slipped under the covers, her mind inevitably drifted to her old life in America. The thought of Daniel and the life she had left behind brought a twinge of anxiety. Was he wondering where she was? Did he even care? Charlotte knew she was on the right path, but the shadow of her old life still loomed large in her mind, casting a pall over her newfound happiness.

She tossed and turned, her thoughts a whirlwind of what-ifs and maybes. She wondered if Daniel was regretting his actions, if he missed her, or if he was moving on without a second thought. A part of her still ached for closure, for some kind of understanding as to why things had fallen apart so completely.

Yet, amid the swirl of emotions and memories, Charlotte found herself smiling at the thought of Simon. There was a simplicity and sincerity about him that was refreshingly different from her life with Daniel. He had shown genuine interest in her dreams, and their conversation had flowed effortlessly, so different from the strained interactions she'd had with her ex-husband in their final months together.

Charlotte knew she was in a liminal space, caught between her past and her future. The journey ahead was uncertain, but for the first time in a long while, she felt hopeful about what was to come. The pain and confusion of her old life were still there, but so was the excitement and potential of her new one. Charlotte clung to the feeling of happiness that her evening with Simon had brought.

For now, she allowed herself the comfort of this small joy, and she drifted into a restless sleep.

CHAPTER FIFTEEN

Charlotte's eyes fluttered open, her mind still swimming in the foggy depths of sleep. She fumbled for her phone on the bedside table, squinting at the glaring screen. The time blinked back at her: 10:15 a.m. A gasp escaped her lips as she realized how late it was. Usually an early riser, Charlotte felt a wave of disorientation wash over her. She rubbed her temples, trying to shake off the grogginess that clung to her like damp cobwebs.

The room, however, offered a balm against the unwelcome chaos of waking up late. A soft morning light filtered through the curtains, casting warm golden hues onto the walls and furniture around her. The plush duvet was weighted over her body, so warm and snuggly that it made parting with it seem like a daunting task. The scent of aged wood and lavender wafted through the air, transporting her to a simpler time.

With a deep breath, Charlotte braced herself to face the day. Despite the rocky start, she felt a sense of peace and belonging within these walls. Just as Charlotte swung her feet over the edge of the bed, a gentle knock on the door heralded Marge's entrance. The older woman appeared in the doorway, balancing a tray laden with a steaming teapot and a plate piled high with golden British biscuits. Her silver hair was swept back into an elegant bun, and her eyes twinkled with motherly warmth.

"Good morning, dear," Marge said, her voice soft and soothing. "I thought you could use a little pick-me-up after your late night." She winked, and Charlotte had the mortifying thought that Marge might have witnessed her near-kiss with Simon.

The aroma of the tea filled the room, mingling with the scent of the freshly baked biscuits. It was an intoxicating blend of bergamot and butter.

"Thank you, Marge," Charlotte said, her heart swelling with gratitude. She hadn't expected such a thoughtful gesture, but it was precisely the kind of care that made The Crown Inn feel like a home away from home.

Marge set the tray down on the bedside table and poured a cup of tea for Charlotte. As she did so, the steam curled up around her face, accentuating the lines etched by time. She handed the cup to Charlotte, who cradled it in her hands, allowing the heat to seep into her fingers.

"Nothing quite like a good cuppa to chase away the morning grogginess," Marge said with a knowing smile. Her gaze lingered on the window, where the sunlight continued to dance across the room.

"Yes, ma'am," Charlotte agreed, taking a tentative sip of the hot liquid. As the tea warmed her insides, she found herself more alert, her thoughts beginning to clear. "This is simply divine, Marge. You must tell me what blend it is."

Marge chuckled softly, a hint of pride in her eyes. "It's my own little secret, dear. But perhaps I'll share it with you before you leave."

"Your secret would be safe with me," Charlotte promised, her curiosity piqued.

As Marge perched on the edge of a nearby armchair with her own tea, the two women sipped their tea in companionable silence. The biscuits were golden and slightly crumbly, their edges tinged with the perfect shade of brown. The faintest hint of sweetness wafted through the air.

"Your biscuits look divine," Charlotte remarked, admiring the artistry and care that had gone into their creation. Charlotte reached for a biscuit. The delicate crumbliness combined with the subtle sweetness created a perfect harmony of flavors, transporting her to a moment of pure bliss.

Marge's face lit up with pride, her chest puffing out ever so slightly. "Thank you, dear. It's an old family recipe passed down through generations," she admitted, the corners of her mouth turning upwards in a contented smile. "Just like this place. My parents left it to me when they passed away, and I've been running it ever since. It's more than just a business to me – it's a part of my family."

As she spoke, Charlotte noticed the way Marge's eyes misted over with emotion.

"Sometimes I worry if I'm doing enough, or if I'm honoring my parents' legacy properly," Marge admitted, looking down at her hands wrapped around her teacup. "But then I get bouts like this – sharing tea and biscuits with someone who appreciates the simple beauty of it all – to remind me that I must be doing something right."

Charlotte reached out to gently touch Marge's arm in reassurance. "The love you have for this place is evident in *every* detail. Your parents would be proud. I'm surprised you're not overrun with guests."

For a moment, the two women returned to companionable silence, sipping their tea and enjoying the peace that enveloped them. To Charlotte, it felt like she was sitting with an old friend, the connection between them growing stronger by the minute. The minutes passed and the tea in their cups diminished, the atmosphere in the room remained warm and comforting. Marge gazed out of the window, her eyes tracing the landscape of Chesham Cove below them. A small frown formed on her face, tugging at the corners of her mouth.

"Charlotte," she began, her voice laced with concern, "I've noticed a change in Chesham Cove over the past few years. There are fewer tourists coming here, and I'm afraid it's affecting our little community."

"Really?" Charlotte asked, concern mirrored in her own expression as she looked out at the picturesque cove. "It seems like such a lovely place. Why do you think that is?"

Marge hesitated for a moment before answering. "I believe it has something to do with Thomas Windnell and his new development down the beach. He's from London proper, and he's built a luxury hotel. It's drawn away many of the visitors who used to come here."

"Ah, I see," Charlotte murmured, her heart aching for Marge.

"Thomas Windnell has approached me several times about buying The Crown Inn," Marge continued, her hands trembling slightly as she clutched her teacup. She seemed to need to tell someone—and Charlotte listened stoically.

"He has grand plans for the cove, but I fear they would only strip it of its character."

"How could he if Chesham Cove is still here? Have you considered selling to him?" Charlotte inquired gently, sensing the turmoil within Marge.

Marge shook her head, her moxie shining through the shadows of her doubts. "No, I couldn't bring myself to do it. My parents worked so hard to build this inn. To sell it to someone like him... it would break my heart."

"I'm sure there must be another solution to bring more tourists back to Chesham Cove without sacrificing its soul."

Marge let out a sigh, her eyes misting over with unshed tears. "I certainly hope so, Charlotte," she whispered, her voice wavering with emotion. "The Crown Inn may not be the grandest establishment in the area, but it's my heart and soul. I just want to see it thrive again. And Windnell has been dropping hints here and there about his plans for Chesham Cove, too. It's all very vague, but I can't help feeling uneasy."

Charlotte's heart skipped a beat, sensing the gravity of the situation. "What kind of hints?" she asked, her voice tinged with apprehension.

"Nothing concrete, mind you," Marge admitted, her gaze distant as she recalled past conversations with the developer. "Just mentions of 'untapped potential' and 'modernizing the community.' But knowing Thomas and what he's done to other places... well, it doesn't bode well for our little corner of the world."

A sudden chill raced down Charlotte's spine, fueled by the foreboding in Marge's words. She couldn't shake the feeling that whatever this Thomas Windnell had in store for Chesham Cove would endanger not only the inn, but also the very essence of the place she'd grown to love so quickly.

"Chesham Cove deserves better than that," Charlotte declared, her voice firm with resolve. "There must be a way to protect it from people like Thomas Windnell."

"From your lips to God's ears, dear," Marge replied, offering a shaky smile that belied the weight of her worries. "Our little cove is full of surprises. And when push comes to shove, we'll do whatever it takes to keep Chesham Cove just as it should be. But who knows if we're the little guys who are *too* little this time, eh?"

"Would you ever consider selling The Crown Inn? To someone else, I mean?" Charlotte asked gently, her curiosity piqued. She hesitated, realizing that it might be too personal a question to ask.

Marge sighed, her eyes reflecting the complexity of her thoughts. "If I'm being honest with you, dear, there have been moments when the thought has crossed my mind," she admitted, her voice wavering slightly. "Not to Thomas Windnell, though, I must impress again. I wouldn't sell to him even if he offered me all the money in the world. But... maybe to someone who truly understands what this place means to me and the community."

Charlotte chewed on her lower lip, deep in thought. Her fingers absently traced the delicate floral pattern of her teacup as she contemplated Marge's words. A part of her wanted to jump at the chance to save the inn, but she knew that she was still figuring out her own life and what direction it was taking. It wasn't the right time for her to make such a commitment, not when she was still healing from her own heartaches and uncertainties.

"Any idea who that someone might be?" Charlotte asked, attempting to keep her tone casual.

Marge shook her head, a touch of sadness in her eyes. "No. But like I said earlier, Chesham Cove is full of surprises. I trust that when the time comes, the right person will come along to carry on the legacy of The Crown."

Charlotte couldn't deny the allure of such a possibility, but now wasn't the time to entertain those thoughts. Instead, she smiled warmly at Marge, grateful for their newfound friendship and determined to wring reclaimed joy out of every moment of her time in Chesham Cove – for however long it might last.

CHAPTER SIXTEEN

Sunlight dappled the cobblestone streets as Charlotte Moore wandered through the charming lanes of Chesham Cove later that day. The quaint architecture and picturesque scenery warmed her heart, bringing a contented smile to her lips. She paused for a moment, drinking in the sight of an ivy-covered cottage nestled amidst a riot of colorful blossoms. This town was the perfect sanctuary for her artistic soul.

As she resumed her leisurely stroll, Charlotte felt the curious glances from some of the locals. Their eyes followed her, intrigued by the presence of this new face in their small town. A few older women in floral dresses exchanged whispers near a bakery, while a gentleman with a weathered cap nodded in her direction before resuming his conversation with a companion on a corner.

"Morning," Charlotte said politely to a middle-aged woman tending to her flower baskets. The woman looked up, surprise flickering across her face before she returned the greeting with a tentative smile.

"Good morning, dear. Are you new here?" she inquired, wiping her hands on her apron.

"Yes, I'm just visiting Chesham Cove," Charlotte replied, her hands clasped behind her back. "Staying at The Crown Inn for now."

"Ah, lovely place, that is," the woman said, nodding in approval. "Margaret is a fine old bird. Well, welcome to our little town. I'm sure you'll love it here."

"Thank you," Charlotte responded, her eyes crinkling with genuine appreciation. "I can already tell this is going to be a wonderful place to call home—for the time being."

With a final wave, Charlotte continued her exploration. She knew that not everyone would be as welcoming as the flower-tending woman, but she refused to let the whispers and stares of a few locals dampen her spirits. This was the fresh start she had been longing for, and Charlotte was determined to make the most of it.

The sun cast long shadows on the cobblestone streets as Charlotte wandered further into the heart of Chesham. Her ears perked up at the sound of tinkling wind chimes and the soft rustle of a sign hanging above a door. Intrigued, she approached the cozy hobby and art supply shop nestled between two ivy-covered buildings.

As Charlotte pushed open the door to the shop, she saw shelves brimming with paints, brushes, and various trinkets. A woman around Charlotte's age stood behind the counter, her vibrant purple hair pulled back in a loose bun, her eyes twinkling like stars as they met Charlotte's gaze.

"Hello there! Welcome to Hobbs' Hobbies," the woman greeted energetically, her voice as warm and inviting as the shop itself. "I'm Samantha Hobbs, owner and resident enthusiast of all things creative."

"Hi, Samantha. I'm Charlotte Anderson," Charlotte replied, extending a hand in greeting. Their fingers met in a firm and friendly shake, solidifying the connection between them.

"Anderson? Huh. Any relation to the local Andersons?" Samantha inquired, her head tilted ever so slightly to one side.

"You know, I'm not sure. But you're not the first to ask that," Charlotte confirmed, a small smile playing on her lips.

"Ah, I see. You must be new here then. I haven't seen you around town before," Samantha said, leaning against the counter with a cheeky grin.

Charlotte nodded, tucking a stray lock of hair behind her ear. "Just arrived a few days ago."

"Welcome to our little slice of heaven." Samantha gestured to the shelves lining the walls. "What brings you to our town?"

"Looking for a change of pace," Charlotte confessed, her fingers tracing the spines of various sketchbooks. "Plus, I've been wanting to focus more on my art. This place seems like the perfect spot to get what I need to paint."

"Ah, an artist! That's wonderful." Samantha's face brightened with genuine interest. "You'll find no shortage of inspiration here, that's for sure. Chesham Cove has its fair share of natural beauty and some charming quirks."

"Any places in particular you'd recommend?" Charlotte asked, glancing up from her perusal of the supplies.

"Definitely the fisherman's wharf down by the shore. It's absolutely picturesque during sunrise and sunset. And there's an old lighthouse not too far off that's a favorite subject of local painters," Samantha suggested, her voice carrying a hint of excitement. "Some fields of wildflowers outside town, and the buildings! I mean, The Crown herself is a lovely building."

"That she is," Charlotte agreed.

Charlotte's fingertips grazed over the rows of oil paints, her eyes drinking in the vibrant hues that lined the shelves. She could already imagine the bold strokes and delicate wisps of color that would soon grace her canvas. The scent of linseed oil and turpentine mingled in the air, the familiar aroma grounding her as she continued to explore the cozy shop.

Her fingers paused at a tube of cerulean blue, an image of the ocean's rolling waves filling her mind's eye. Selecting a number of high-quality paints from the display, she eagerly envisioned the sunsets and rugged cliffs she would soon commit to canvas.

Next, she perused the brushes, carefully considering their bristles and handles, seeking the perfect tools to translate her vision into reality. Finally settling on a few sable-hair brushes of varying sizes, she placed them alongside the paints in her basket.

"Canvases are just around the corner," Samantha pointed out, sensing Charlotte's next need. "We have a variety of sizes and materials to choose from, depending on your preference."

"Thank you," Charlotte murmured, her gaze sweeping over the blank canvases that awaited her. She selected a few sturdy, already stretched linen canvases, their crisp white surfaces waiting for her untold stories and creative expressions.

"Looks like you've gathered quite the collection there," Samantha remarked, a smile playing on her lips as she observed Charlotte's choices.

"Here's to hoping," Charlotte replied. She made her way to the register.

As Samantha rang up Charlotte's selections, she casually leaned against the counter and said, "You know, we have quite a creative community here in Chesham Cove. There are regular art workshops at the community center, and a small but passionate group of artists who gather for plein air painting sessions by the harbor."

Charlotte listened intently, her fingers absently tracing the smooth handles of the brushes as she envisioned herself joining these artists, capturing the beauty of the cove on canvas. She felt a spark of excitement at the prospect of immersing herself in the local art scene, allowing it to nurture her talent and inspire new ideas. She had lived in New York her whole life, and she'd *never* painted alongside another artist outside of school.

How isolated she had been—even in that bustling place.

"Sounds lovely," she murmured, a soft smile playing on her lips. "I've been looking for an opportunity to meet other artists and learn from them. It's been too long since I've had that kind of camaraderie."

Samantha grinned, her eyes twinkling with enthusiasm. "And if you're ever interested in trying something new, I offer classes here at the shop as well. We dabble in everything from watercolors to pottery. Bet you could teach oil painting, couldn't you?"

"Really?" Charlotte asked, her curiosity piqued. She imagined the cozy shop transforming into a lively studio space, filled with laughter, learning, and the scent of wet paint mingling with the earthy aroma of clay.

"Absolutely!" Samantha confirmed, nodding enthusiastically. "In fact, we have a watercolor workshop coming up next week. You should join us! Just pop in, see what's what."

"Thank you," she said softly, her gratitude evident in her warm gaze. "I'd love to join you."

Samantha beamed, her cheeks flushing with happiness. "It's been a pleasure meeting you, Charlotte. Welcome to Chesham Cove. We're lucky to have you here."

With a final exchange of smiles, Charlotte gathered her new art supplies and stepped back outside the cozy hobby shop. She took a deep breath of the crisp spring air, feeling the cool breeze brush against her cheeks like a gentle caress. She knew exactly what she wanted to do now.

She wanted to paint The Crown Inn—and that was exactly what she was going to do.

CHAPTER SEVENTEEN

Charlotte stood in the yard of The Crown, her fingers eagerly touching the new, smooth wooden handle of her paint brush. The sun was shining overhead, casting perfectly angled rays of light that danced through the leaves of the surrounding trees and illuminated patches of lush grass beneath her feet. A gentle breeze rustled the branches above.

As Charlotte began to unpack her new supplies, she took a moment to appreciate the serenity of the scene before her. The inn seemed to be in perfect harmony with the natural world around it. The weathered brick walls and ivy-covered facade spoke to a history rich with stories, and the slightly crooked windows only added to its charm.

Birds sang their melodies from hidden perches, providing a soothing soundtrack. The yard itself was a treasure trove of inspiration for Charlotte's wandering artist's eye. A low stone wall separated the inn's property from the neighboring meadow, adorned with moss and wildflowers that seemed to grow from the very cracks between the stones. An old oak tree cast its shade over a corner of the yard, inviting visitors to rest beneath its vast canopy and lose themselves in daydreams. The vibrant colors and textures of the scene beckoned Charlotte, urging her to capture the beauty on her canvas.

As she set up her easel and carefully arranged her brushes and paints, Charlotte could feel her excitement building. She knew that this place held something special, and she couldn't wait to immortalize it in her art. With each stroke of her brush, she would not only be painting the inn and its surroundings, but she would also be capturing the essence of a life she had only just begun to explore.

As Charlotte carefully lifted her paint tubes from the Hobbs' Hobbies bag, her pulse quickened with anticipation. The colors spread before her like a vibrant rainbow – deep cadmium reds, warm ochres, and cool cerulean blues. She inhaled deeply, savoring the potent smell of oil paints mingling with the scent of freshly cut grass.

"Ah, the joy of a fresh canvas," she mused to herself as she gingerly slid her fingertips across the pristine surface, feeling the slightly rough texture that would soon be filled with color and life.

Charlotte selected a few brushes from her collection, each one an extension of her creative hand. She ran her fingers through the bristles, feeling their soft tips, knowing that soon they would dance across the canvas, creating magic with every stroke. Taking a moment to center herself, Charlotte closed her eyes and took a slow, deep breath. She could feel the sun warming her face, the gentle breeze rustling her hair, and the symphony of nature that surrounded her. She opened her eyes, dipped her chosen brush into a small dollop of paint, and brought it to the canvas with a steady hand.

As she began to lay down the first strokes of color, Charlotte felt herself fitting together with the scene before her, as if each brushstroke was weaving her deeper into the fabric of this idyllic place. With every dab and stroke of pigment, she could feel her excitement growing.

Charlotte stepped back, surveying the yard as she considered the best angle to capture the inn's charm. The aged bricks? The vines that crept along its walls? Both softened the lines of time etched into the building.

"Perhaps from here," she mused aloud, moving her easel and canvas toward the corner, where the garden met the cobblestone path. She adjusted the height and angle of the easel before stepping back once more, squinting her eyes to envision the final outcome.

"Perfect," Charlotte whispered, a small smile playing on her lips as she turned her attention to the inn itself.

With the focus and concentration of an artist determined to do justice to her subject, Charlotte studied every detail – the way the window shutters framed the worn glass, the intricate carvings adorning the eaves, and the inviting entrance that beckoned visitors to step inside.

The sunlight shifted, casting new shadows and revealing previously unnoticed elements, like the tiny chip in the paint on the front door. Charlotte thought of her own house—the paint chip on the doorframe. And as she painted, Charlotte knew she was not only capturing the inn's essence but also finding her own place within its walls and the hearts of those who called it home.

Was there a place here for her?

With a deep breath, Charlotte steadied her hand and dipped her brush into the soft gray paint. The initial brushstrokes were cautious, yet purposeful, as she outlined the shape of the inn's roof and walls. She continued to build on this foundation, adding windows and doors, each stroke imbuing the canvas with the essence of the historic building. As she worked, her thoughts wandered back to the day she first arrived at the inn, seeking solace from the painful collapse of her marriage. Painting the inn felt like an homage to the nascent healing it had brought her.

As Charlotte added details to the eaves and shutters, her thoughts drifted to the people she'd met during her stay. Each interaction, whether it was sharing a cup of tea with Marge or swapping stories with Simon, had been an opportunity to grow beyond her past. She carefully painted the delicate tendrils winding their way up the side of the inn. She imagined the years of growth and change the ivy had witnessed, much like herself.

As the painting took shape, Charlotte felt a sense of fulfillment and gratitude wash over her. The inn was now a symbol of her resilience, her growth. She could feel the bristles' gentle resistance against the canvas, leaving behind streaks of color that seemed to breathe life into her painting. Each stroke felt like an extension of herself, her emotions pouring out and merging with the hues on the canvas.

As the hours passed, the painting continued to evolve under Charlotte's skilled hand. She occasionally stepped back, her eyes scanning the canvas critically, making adjustments and refining details as needed.

Charlotte dipped her brush into the vibrant red paint, and she began to add depth and texture to the inn's brick walls. The crimson hue blended seamlessly with the soft beige mortar, each stroke capturing the character of the old building. With each layer of color and detail, the inn seemed to come alive. Charlotte skillfully applied highlights to the windows, giving them a warm glow that seemed to beckon passersby inside. The lush greenery surrounding the building appeared to sway gently in the breeze, and even the cobblestone pathway seemed worn and well-trodden.

As Charlotte neared the completion of the portrait, she was overcome by a sense of satisfaction and accomplishment unlike any she'd ever experienced. It wasn't just the physical act of painting that brought her joy, but the knowledge that she had managed to capture the essence of a place that had come to mean so much to her. With the final brushstroke applied, Charlotte felt a deep sense of fulfillment wash over her.

It was then that Charlotte realized—she didn't want to go back to New York.

She didn't know if she *ever* wanted to go back.

Oh, my.
Charlotte needed some advice, and fast.

CHAPTER EIGHTEEN

Charlotte's fingers trembled slightly as she picked up her phone, the device feeling heavier than usual in her hand. Her heart pounded in her chest as she dialed Roxanne's number, a mix of anxiety and excitement coursing through her veins. She bit her lip nervously, mentally rehearsing what she wanted to say.

"Come on, Roxy, pick up," Charlotte whispered under her breath, eyes fixated on the screen as it continued to show the call connecting. The familiar buzzing sound of the dial tone hummed in her ear, providing an uneasy soundtrack to her mounting anticipation.

As she waited for Roxanne to answer, Charlotte reflected on the fact that she had bought a one-way ticket to Chesham Cove without even considering the possibility of returning. The realization sent a surge of uncertainty and doubt rushing through her like a tidal wave, momentarily threatening to overwhelm her.

Why had she been so impulsive? What if this entire journey was a mistake? Or had she meant it—what if she had meant it? The questions swirled around her mind like leaves caught in a whirlwind, refusing to settle.

"Deep breaths, Charlotte," she reminded herself, inhaling slowly and deliberately in an attempt to regain control over her racing thoughts. She could almost hear Roxanne's voice in her head, chiding her for her tendency to overthink things and encouraging her to trust herself.

"Remember, you're stronger than you think," she could imagine her sister saying. And as the words echoed through her consciousness, a small smile tugged at the corners of her lips. If anyone could understand what she was going through and offer guidance, it was Roxanne.

The heavy weight of concern began to lighten somewhat, replaced with a flicker of hope. No matter the outcome of her search, Charlotte knew she could rely on her sister. And with that thought, she braced herself for the conversation to come, anxiously waiting for Roxanne to answer the call.

"Hey, Char! How's England treating you?" Roxanne's voice crackled through the line, a familiar and comforting sound that instantly put Charlotte at ease.

"Rox, it's absolutely incredible," Charlotte gushed, her apprehension momentarily forgotten as she eagerly began recounting her experiences in Chesham Cove. "The Crown Inn is just like something out of a storybook – all ivy-covered walls and cozy fireplaces. And Marge, the owner, is such a wonderful woman. She's really gone out of her way to make me feel welcome."

"Everyone I've met so far has been so friendly and kind," she continued, her words painting a vivid picture of the close-knit community. "It's almost like stepping back in time – life here seems so much simpler, slower-paced, and more meaningful."

Despite her enthusiasm, however, there was an underlying current of uncertainty that pulsed beneath the surface of her narrative – a subtle tremor that hinted at the deeper reason for her call. As she paused to catch her breath, Charlotte hesitated for a moment before taking the plunge, her voice trembling slightly as she broached the subject that weighed most heavily on her heart.

"Rox, there's something I need to tell you," she admitted, swallowing hard as she forced the words past the lump in her throat. "I've been thinking of doing some digging, with Marge's help, and... I think I might find some family here. You know, on Dad's side. And that means I'll stay here a bit longer."

The silence that followed was heavy with anticipation, as if the world around her had suddenly been plunged into a state of suspended animation. Charlotte could feel her heart pounding in her chest, each beat like the tolling of a distant bell echoing through the void.

"Are you sure?" Roxanne's voice cut through the stillness, her tone laced with surprise and curiosity. "How will you find them?"

"Internet ancestry websites, mainly," Charlotte replied, her fingers fidgeting nervously with the hem of her shirt as she explained the painstaking process of piecing together fragments of information from various sources. "It's not a hundred percent certain yet, but... if I find them, I really want to reach out to them, Rox."

"Of course you do," Roxanne responded gently, her words like a balm to Charlotte's frazzled nerves. "And I think you should stay as long as you need to."

"Okay," Charlotte whispered, grateful beyond words for her sister's support and reassurance. "I just... I don't know what to say to them or even how to approach it."

"Start simple – reach out, introduce yourself, and explain your connection," Roxanne suggested. "The key is to be open and honest. I have faith in you, Char."

"Alright," Charlotte murmured, her determination solidifying. "I'll try."

"Good. And remember, I'm your first call for any gossip, family drama, or discovery that we have a large, lost inheritance."

Charlotte laughed, and with a final word of encouragement, Roxanne ended the call, leaving Charlotte staring at her phone, the instrument of their connection now silent.

***

That afternoon, Charlotte opened her laptop and began her search, following Marge's advice and assistance from earlier about where Chesham's local Andersons were located.

She typed the names of the potential relatives into the search bar, her fingers tapping lightly on the keys as she waited for the results to load. As each page materialized before her, Charlotte felt a thrill of anticipation mixed with trepidation, her heart fluttering like a caged bird within her chest.

"Okay, here goes," she whispered to herself, her eyes scanning the screen for any hint of a connection.

She clicked on the first link and began to read, determined to find the missing pieces of her family history. Charlotte's fingers hovered above her keyboard, the letters M-A-R-I-O-N staring back at her from the screen. This was it. A potential relative who could provide answers about her family history. Maybe about Henry—her father. Charlotte's heart pounded in her ears as she took a deep breath and clicked on the link to Marion's contact information. Her eyes widened at the sight of the phone number, suddenly all too real.

"Okay, Charlotte," she whispered to herself, attempting to steady her trembling hands. "You've come this far. You can do this."

She picked up the phone and entered the digits slowly, deliberately, each tone echoing in her ears like the distant tolling of a bell. She hesitated before pressing the call button, memories of Roxanne's encouragement flooding her mind. With one last steadying breath, she pressed the button and brought the phone to her ear.

The phone rang once, twice, the sound sending shivers down Charlotte's spine. Her stomach twisted into anxious knots as she paced the confines of her room, her feet sinking into the plush carpet with each step. The anticipation was palpable, the air around her seeming to hum with an electric energy that threatened to overwhelm her senses.

"Come on," she murmured, gripping the phone tightly. "Please answer."

As the phone continued to ring, Charlotte's thoughts raced. What if Marion wasn't home? What if she didn't want to talk to Charlotte? Or worse, what if she wasn't related to her at all? The doubt gnawed at the edges of her courage, but she refused to let it consume her.

"Roxanne is right," she reminded herself silently, her gaze fixed on the old photograph of her parents resting on her bedside table. "I am strong. I am resilient. And I deserve to know the truth."

Her heart leaped in her chest as the ringing finally stopped, replaced by the faint sound of breathing on the other end of the line. She had made contact – now, all that remained was to see if Marion would open the door to the past and help Charlotte find the answers she so desperately sought.

"Hello?" Charlotte queried tentatively, unsure if the breathing she heard was indeed her potential relative. But just as she spoke those words, the line went dead, leaving her with nothing but a sharp tone in her ear and a sinking feeling in the pit of her stomach.

"Wait!" she exclaimed, though she knew there was no one left to hear her plea. A mix of disappointment and confusion washed over her like a cold wave on an autumn day. Had she dialed the wrong number? Or perhaps it had been the right number, but something had spooked Marion into ending the call so abruptly.

"Focus, Charlotte," she whispered to herself, her fingers gripping the edge of the heavy wooden desk in front of her. "You can't give up now."

Taking a deep breath, she steadied her trembling hands and carefully entered the digits of another potential relative's phone number. Her heart raced, pounding in her chest like it was desperate to break free from its confines.

The phone rang once, twice, and then a third time. With each ring, Charlotte's hope began to wane, threatening to slip through her fingers like sand through an hourglass. She clenched her jaw, determined not to let the fear consume her as it had done so many times in the past.

"Hello?" a voice answered, soft yet strong, pulling Charlotte back from the precipice of despair.

"Um, hi," she stuttered, momentarily taken aback by the sudden response. "My name is Charlotte Moore... Anderson. I'm trying to find my family, and I think we might be related. Is this Evelyn?"

"Charlotte?" the voice on the other end repeated, a hint of curiosity mingling with surprise. "Well, I'll be darned. Yes, this is Evelyn. How can I help you, dear?"

The warmth in Evelyn's voice wrapped around Charlotte like a comforting embrace, breathing new life into her desire to solve the mystery of her past. She had found another potential relative – perhaps, this time, she would finally uncover the truth that had eluded her for so long.

"Thank you," Charlotte replied, her voice choked with emotion. "I'm just trying to piece together my family history, and I think you might have some answers I've been searching for."

"Of course, dear," Evelyn said kindly. "That sounds nice."

The line went dead, leaving nothing but a hollow silence that echoed in Charlotte's ear. She stared at the phone, her heart sinking with each passing second as she tried to process what had just happened. Had Evelyn hung up on her? Was it a simple misunderstanding, or had she inadvertently struck a nerve?

She tried the number again, but it just rang and rang.

"Maybe it's not meant to be," she murmured, running her fingers through her chestnut hair. Charlotte glanced around the cozy sitting room of Marge's inn, taking in the warm hues of the wallpaper, the soft glow from the table lamp, and the delicate ticking of the grandfather clock in the corner.

"Come on, Charlotte," she whispered, steeling herself for one final attempt. "You've come too far to give up now."

Her fingers trembling slightly, she dialed the number of the third potential family member, her pulse quickening. Marge had left her with a list of possible relatives, and this was the last name: Agnes.

"Please," she prayed silently, "let this be the one."

As the phone rang, Charlotte's breath hitched in her chest. The familiar doubts began to creep in, casting shadows. What if Agnes didn't want to speak with her? What if she was opening old wounds that were better left untouched?

"Enough," she scolded herself, banishing the negative thoughts and focusing on the sound of the ringing phone. This was her chance, her opportunity to finally uncover the truth and connect with her long-lost family.

And she wouldn't let fear stand in her way.

The ringing seemed to stretch on for an eternity, the sound resonating within Charlotte's chest. Just as she was about to give in to despair, the call connected, and Charlotte introduced herself.

A cheerful voice emerged from the other end. "Hello? Is this Henry's Charlotte?"

Charlotte froze, her breath catching in her throat. She hadn't expected someone to know her connection to Henry right away. Gathering her wits, she managed to stammer out a response. "Y-yes, it's me. I'm Charlotte."

"Ah, my dear, I thought so!" Agnes exclaimed with genuine warmth. "I'm your cousin Agnes, on your father's side. Marge told me you were trying to reach me – she's such a dear."

A cozy feeling encircled Charlotte, as if she were wrapped in a soft, familiar blanket. The welcoming tone of Agnes's voice instantly put her at ease, and she found herself smiling despite the uncertainty that had been plaguing her. "It's so nice to finally speak with you, Agnes," she said, her voice gaining strength. "I've been searching for my father's family, hoping to learn more about him and our heritage."

"Of course, my dear, I understand completely. It must have been quite a journey for you to come all the way to Chesham Cove." There was a comforting maternal quality to Agnes's words, one that Charlotte hadn't realized she'd been craving.

"Would you like to join me for tea tomorrow afternoon?" Agnes offered suddenly, her voice laced with excitement. "I'd love to get to know you better and share what I can about our family history."

Charlotte hesitated for a moment, feeling vulnerable but also eager to meet her newfound relative. She could sense the sincerity in Agnes's invitation, and the prospect of finally finding answers was too enticing to resist. "I'd be delighted to join you," she replied, her heart swelling with a renewed sense of hope and connection.

"Marvelous! I'll message you my address. I'm looking forward to our chat, Charlotte."

"Thank you, Agnes," Charlotte said softly, touched by the genuine warmth and kindness she heard in her cousin's voice. "I'll see you tomorrow."

As she ended the call, Charlotte stared at the phone in her hand, feeling a mixture of disbelief and elation. She had finally found a family member who seemed eager to connect with her, someone who could shed light on her father's past and help her understand where she came from.

The shadows of doubt receded, replaced by a warm glow that filled her chest. In that moment, as the grandfather clock continued its gentle ticking, Charlotte felt more at home than ever before.

Charlotte sat there for a moment, cradling the device in her hand. Her heart thudded in her chest, anticipation and curiosity growing within her like vines reaching for the sun. The room seemed to hum with energy, as if it sensed the significance of this new connection. Tomorrow's meeting loomed large in her imagination, a door opening onto a world of possibilities.

Outside, the wind brushed against the windowpanes, whispering secrets that only the trees could understand. Charlotte's thoughts wandered to the conversation that lay ahead, hidden treasures waiting to be discovered. She envisioned faded photographs and worn letters, tender moments and shared laughter, all the memories that had been lost to time but not forgotten.

She rose from the armchair, feeling lighter than she had in years, as if the weight of her unanswered questions had been lifted ever so slightly. A tentative smile played at the corners of her mouth as she moved toward the window, where the last rays of sunlight painted the clouds in shades of gold and lavender.

"Charlotte," she murmured, testing the sound of her name on her lips like a talisman. "Henry's Charlotte."

Her thoughts danced around the unknowns of tomorrow's meeting. What would Agnes be like? How much did she know about their shared past? For now, those questions remained unanswered, suspended in the air like fireflies.

"Finally," Charlotte breathed, her voice barely audible even to herself. "I might find the missing pieces."

And maybe—what if it turned out that Agnes knew where Henry was?

She needed a distraction, and she couldn't call Roxanne again. Maybe a little trip to the harbor was in order.

CHAPTER NINETEEN

Charlotte's heart raced with anticipation as she made her way to the harbor, her mind buzzing with thoughts of Simon. She had been looking forward to this moment all day, eager to "casually" run into Simon and see his rugged, handsome face once more. It was a warm afternoon in Chesham Cove, perfect for a walk.

As she approached the harbor, Charlotte was greeted by the bustling activity of fishermen unloading their catch for the day. The salty air mingled with the scent of fresh fish, carried along by a gentle sea breeze. Seagulls soared overhead, their raucous cries filling the air as they swooped down to snatch any morsel they could find.

Charlotte's eyes scanned the docks, searching for Simon among the busy fishermen. Her heart pounded a little faster with each step she took, her excitement growing as she drew nearer to the water's edge. She could almost picture him there, his strong hands expertly navigating his boat through the waves, his sun-kissed skin glinting in the sunlight.

The sound of laughter and chatter filled the harbor as fishermen exchanged stories of their latest catches and discussed plans for the evening. It was a lively scene that Charlotte was drawn to, even as her thoughts remained preoccupied with Simon.

A flurry of seagulls dove and swooped around the fishing boats, their cacophony of squawks blending with the fishermen's jovial banter. Charlotte inhaled deeply, absorbing the salty scent of the ocean mingled with fish, seaweed, and the faint aroma of fresh bread from a nearby bakery. She hoped that Simon would be among the sea-hardy fishermen unloading their catch at the harbor.

Her eyes darted from one boat to another, heart skipping a beat each time she thought she found his. But so far, Simon's familiar vessel eluded her. The vibrant colors of the boats bobbed gently on the water as they kissed the edge of the dock, their names painted boldly on their hulls. She chewed her lip in anticipation, her gaze continuing to search.

"Come on, Simon," she muttered under her breath, fingers drumming against her thigh in an anxious rhythm. "Where are you?"

As if answering her silent plea, a weathered boat with peeling paint carved its way through the sparkling waves, steering toward the dock. The name 'The Mariner' was emblazoned across its side, and as it drew closer, Charlotte recognized Simon's strong figure at the helm. His windswept hair danced in the breeze, and he maneuvered the boat with practiced ease.

"Ah, there you are," she whispered, her heart doing a somersault in her chest. A smile tugged at the corners of her mouth as excitement surged through her veins. Relief washed over her, like the tide kissing the shore – though maybe she shouldn't be thinking of kissing, after that embarrassing faux pas the other night.

Charlotte stared at him as he deftly steered his boat into position alongside the dock. Her pulse raced, warmth spreading across her cheeks. She clutched her hands together, trying to contain the giddiness that threatened to bubble over.

"Okay, Charlotte," she thought, taking a deep breath. "Stay calm. You can do this. Just be casual."

As Simon's boat came to a gentle stop, Charlotte felt her excitement reach new heights. She couldn't wait to see his sun-kissed face up close once more and exchange playful banter with the rugged fisherman who had captivated her heart. As Simon secured the boat to the dock, his green eyes met Charlotte's, and a playful grin appeared on his face. He stepped onto the wooden planks, closing the distance between them with effortless confidence.

"Charlotte," he greeted her warmly, his voice as smooth as the sea that surrounded them. "What a surprise to see you here. I had no idea you were so interested in the local fishing industry."

Simon's teasing tone sent a shiver down Charlotte's spine, and she felt a blush creep up her cheeks. She met his gaze head-on, determined not to let him get the better of her.

"Simon, I didn't realize you had an exclusive claim to this area," she retorted playfully, her eyes sparkling with mischief. "Besides, I'm merely appreciating the beauty of Chesham Cove. It's a shame it took me so long to find it."

"Ah, yes," Simon chuckled, crossing his arms over his broad chest. "The beauty of the cove. That must be why you're standing here, watching the boats with such... intensity."

Charlotte laughed, her heart skipping a beat at his teasing. She knew he was onto her little scheme, but she refused to back down. Instead, she arched an eyebrow and shot him a coy smile.

"Can you blame me?" she asked, her voice barely above a whisper. "The sight of a skilled fisherman at work is quite mesmerizing, don't you think?"

"Is that so?" Simon murmured, taking a step closer, his green eyes twinkling with amusement. "Well, in that case, I should invite you to observe more often. It's not every day I receive such high praise."

"Perhaps I will," Charlotte replied, her heartbeat quickening as their playful banter continued. "I have a feeling there's a lot more to learn about Chesham Cove and its charming fishermen."

"Indeed, there is," Simon agreed, his voice low and inviting. "But really, the interesting fisherman count is very limited. To one. There's only one that's worth the bother."

Their eyes locked, and for a moment, time seemed to stand still. The hustle and bustle of the harbor faded to a distant hum, leaving only the tension between them.

"Speaking of learning more," Simon began, his voice laced with anticipation, "how would you feel about joining me for dinner tonight? I know a lovely little place just up the coast that serves the best seafood in town."

Charlotte's eyes widened, and she felt a surge of excitement course through her. Her heart raced at the thought of spending more time with Simon, their connection undeniable even in the few moments they had shared.

"Tonight?" she asked, trying to keep her voice steady despite the butterflies in her stomach. "I'd love to, Simon." She paused, glancing down at her watch. "What time should I be ready?"

"Let's say around seven?" Simon suggested, his green eyes warm and inviting. "That should give us enough time to enjoy the sunset while we're having our meal."

"Seven sounds perfect," Charlotte agreed. She couldn't remember the last time she had looked forward to something so much. The anticipation of their evening together made her feel alive.

"Great," Simon grinned, seemingly as thrilled as she was. "I'll pick you up at your INN, then. It's a date. A second date."

"Sounds lovely," Charlotte murmured, her heart swelling with joy as Simon turned to leave, giving her one last lingering look before he disappeared onto his boat.

As he walked away, Charlotte could hardly contain her excitement. She knew she was taking a risk by agreeing to go on a second date with Simon. Yet, something inside her told her it was worth it – that he was worth it. It was as if fate had led her to Chesham Cove, to this rugged fisherman who had already stolen a piece of her heart.

***

Later that day, Charlotte found herself at a local car rental agency, feeling the need for a set of wheels to take herself to Agnes's place. The anticipation of her evening with Simon only added to the sense of adventure she felt.

"Here you are, Miss Moore," the cheerful rental agent said, handing over the keys to a small but sturdy-looking car. "You're all set."

"Thank you," Charlotte replied, her fingers closing around the cool metal of the keyring. Taking a deep breath, she approached the vehicle, trying to steel her nerves. After all, she reasoned, driving on the opposite side of the road couldn't be that difficult, could it?

As she slid into the driver's seat, however, her confidence wavered. Everything felt so foreign – the steering wheel was on the right, the gearshift on her left, and even the pedals seemed slightly off. Adjusting the mirrors with trembling hands, she tried to quell the butterflies fluttering in the pit of her stomach.

"Okay, Charlotte," she whispered to herself, gripping the steering wheel tightly as if it were a lifeline. "You've got this. Just take it slow, and you'll be fine."

With a determined nod, Charlotte turned the key in the ignition and shifted the car into gear. Her grip on the steering wheel tightened as she haltingly ventured out of the rental agency's lot and onto the winding English road.

"Alright, just remember: left side, left side," she muttered to herself while cautiously navigating the bends and turns, her knuckles white from clutching the wheel. At one point, she found herself veering uncomfortably close to the edge of the road, eliciting an alarmed honk from an oncoming driver. Heart pounding, she quickly corrected her course, offering an apologetic wave to the disgruntled motorist.

"Sorry!" she called out, cheeks flushing with embarrassment. "Still getting used to this."

Gradually, however, Charlotte began to settle into the rhythm of the drive, her anxiety ebbing away as she took in the lush, rolling countryside. The verdant hills stretched out before her, dotted with picturesque stone cottages and the occasional flock of sheep contentedly grazing on the emerald grass.

But suddenly, rounding a bend, Charlotte was confronted by a sea of fluffy white bodies blocking her path. She managed to brake, and then stared in disbelief as the flock of sheep seemed to have taken over the entire road, their bleating cacophony filling the air.

"Are you kidding me?" she groaned, slapping a hand to her forehead.

In a mild panic, she honked the horn, hoping it would encourage the woolly creatures to move aside. Instead, they merely blinked at her with placid expressions, seemingly unperturbed by the noise.

"Come on, shoo! I've got places to be!" Charlotte pleaded through the open window, waving her hands frantically in an attempt to disperse the stubborn animals. "Please?"

The sheep continued to stare at her, unmoving, as if challenging her to find another way around their impromptu roadblock. Charlotte sighed, glancing at the narrow strip of grassy shoulder beside the road, then back at the sheep.

"Fine," she huffed, rolling up her sleeves and setting her jaw. "If you won't move for me, then I'll just have to move you myself."

With that, Charlotte stepped out of the car and approached the flock, her hands on her hips. She tried her best to imitate a stern, authoritative tone as she addressed them.

"Move it!"

They stared, immobile.

Charlotte pursed her lips. Maybe she needed to speak their language.

"Alright, *you lot*," she said firmly, pointing down the road. "I need you to *clear off* and let me pass, please. Now, be good sheep and move along."

To her surprise, the woolly horde began to part slowly, as if considering her request. A bemused smile tugged at the corners of her lips as she watched the animals finally shuffle off the road, allowing her access once more.

"Thank you," she called out with a chuckle, shaking her head in disbelief. Returning to the driver's seat, she felt a sense of accomplishment – not only had she managed to overcome her initial fears of driving in a foreign country, but she had also successfully negotiated with a flock of uncooperative sheep.

"Unbelievable," she murmured with a grin, shaking her head. With a sigh of relief, she eased the car back onto the roadway, carefully navigating around the lingering sheep who cast curious glances in her direction.

The countryside scenery provided a pleasant distraction for Charlotte, easing her nerves bit by bit as she grew more comfortable with the foreign driving conditions. The verdant landscape stretched out on either side of the road, punctuated by the occasional charming cottage or grazing livestock.

"Can't believe I'm actually doing this," she mused, feeling a giddy surge of pride at her newfound confidence.

As the miles slipped away beneath the tires, Charlotte's anticipation began to rise once more. She would soon be meeting Agnes, her cousin, and an important connection to the past she was so eager to uncover. Thoughts raced through her mind – would Agnes be welcoming? Would she be able to shed light on the mysteries that had drawn Charlotte to Chesham Cove in the first place?

Before she knew it, Charlotte found herself turning onto a narrow gravel driveway lined with wildflowers that danced in the gentle breeze. The car rolled to a stop in front of a quaint stone cottage nestled among lush gardens. A warm, inviting glow emanated from the windows, beckoning her inside.

CHAPTER TWENTY

Charlotte's hands trembled slightly as she stood at the gate, her eyes taking in the cozy cottage nestled in the lush countryside of Chesham Cove. The fragrance of wildflowers permeated the air, a soft melody of birdsong filling her ears. This was Agnes Darling's home, the woman who held the key to unlocking a part of Charlotte's past that had been hidden from her for far too long.

With a deep breath, she pushed open the creaking gate and walked up the stone pathway toward the front door. The rhythmic crunch of gravel beneath her feet seemed to mark her journey toward understanding – an understanding of her estranged father, Henry Anderson.

As she raised her hand to knock on the door, she felt a mixture of anticipation and apprehension fluttering in her chest. She knew that this conversation might unravel secrets long buried, but it was a risk she was willing to take.

No sooner had her knuckles rapped against the wooden door, it swung open to reveal Agnes, her warm smile as inviting as the golden sunlight bathing the countryside. "Charlotte! How lovely to finally meet you," Agnes exclaimed, reaching out to envelop her in a welcoming embrace.

"Thank you for having me," Charlotte replied, her voice wavering slightly with nerves as she followed Agnes inside.

"Of course, dear. I'm so glad you came. Would you like a cup of tea?" Agnes asked, motioning toward the kitchen where a pot was already steaming on the stove.

"Tea would be lovely, thank you," Charlotte answered, grateful for the familiar ritual. As she took a seat at the small wooden table, her mind raced with questions, her heart aching for answers.

Agnes poured two cups of tea, the fragrant steam spiraling upwards as she handed one to Charlotte. "I hope you don't mind Earl Grey," she said with a gentle smile.

"Earl Grey is my favorite," Charlotte replied, cradling the warm porcelain in her hands. She took a sip of tea and closed her eyes for a moment, allowing the familiar taste to ground her. This was the beginning of a conversation that might lead to life-changing things. And though she was uncertain of what lay ahead, she knew that she couldn't turn back now.

"Charlotte, I know you must have a lot on your mind," Agnes began softly, acknowledging the weight of their meeting, "I'm here to help you in any way I can."

"Thank you, Agnes," Charlotte murmured, her voice filled with gratitude and hope. The road to understanding her father's mysterious past might be long and winding, but at least now, she had an ally by her side.

"Come, let me show you the living room," Agnes said, her warm smile never leaving her face as she led Charlotte down a narrow hallway. The scent of lavender filled the air, mingling with the lingering aroma of Earl Grey tea that still clung to their fingertips.

As they entered the cozy space, Charlotte's gaze immediately fell upon the walls adorned with family photos. The faces of Agnes's son and daughter smiled back at her.

"Your children are beautiful," Charlotte remarked, her eyes scanning each photo in turn, searching for any resemblance to her own features.

"Thank you," Agnes replied, her expression tender as she followed Charlotte's gaze. "That's my son, Harold, and my daughter, Emily."

"Harold is an architect," Agnes shared with a hint of pride in her voice, pointing toward a picture of a tall, dark-haired man holding a blueprint. "He helped design some of the restored buildings in Chesham Cove's town center."

"Really?" Charlotte asked, her interest piqued. She had always admired the quaint charm of the town's architecture, and discovering this connection to her newfound family made it all the more special.

"Emily, on the other hand, is a botanist," Agnes continued, gesturing to a photograph of a woman with long, wavy hair, surrounded by lush greenery. "She travels the world, studying rare plants and their medicinal properties."

"Wow," Charlotte breathed, genuinely impressed. As an artist herself, she could appreciate the dedication and passion required to pursue one's dreams. She found herself yearning to learn more about these individuals who were, in some way, connected to her own story.

"Tell me more about them," Charlotte urged, her eyes meeting Agnes's, filled with curiosity and longing.

"Of course," Agnes said warmly, settling into an armchair as Charlotte took a seat on the plush sofa. The late afternoon light continued to stream through the windows, casting a warm glow upon the room as if to embrace the conversation that unfolded.

Agnes began to weave tales of her children's lives, painting vivid images of their accomplishments and the joy they brought to her heart. She described Harold's unwavering determination as he worked tirelessly to create beautiful, functional spaces for the community. She spoke of Emily's fascination with the natural world, her desire to protect and preserve the earth's most precious treasures.

As Charlotte listened intently to each story, she felt a pang of envy. These were the memories she had missed out on—stories of family love and support that had never been a part of her own upbringing. Both of her parents had been loving, but distant—busy, always struggling. And yet, she couldn't deny the warmth that swathed her as Agnes spoke, drawing her further into the tapestry of their shared history.

"Your children are truly remarkable," Charlotte finally whispered, her voice tinged with awe and appreciation. "You must be so proud."

"I am," Agnes replied softly, her eyes glistening with unshed tears. "But I believe there is greatness within all of us, Charlotte, including you."

A gentle breeze rustled the curtains, carrying with it the scents of wildflowers and freshly cut grass. Charlotte inhaled deeply, allowing the familiar smells to ground her as she gathered her thoughts. The stories Agnes shared about her children had stirred a longing within Charlotte, and as much as she was enjoying their newfound connection, she knew that she couldn't leave without asking the question that weighed heavily on her heart.

"Agnes," Charlotte began, her voice hesitant and filled with vulnerability. "I've been wanting to ask you about my father, Henry." She paused, her fingers nervously playing with the fabric of her skirt. "Have you seen him recently?"

Agnes studied her for a moment, her eyes searching Charlotte's face, as if trying to gauge the depth of her curiosity. Her expression softened, and she reached out to take Charlotte's hand, offering a warm squeeze of reassurance.

"Charlotte, dear," she said gently. "I can't lie to you. I have seen him from time to time, though his visits are few and far between. Maybe every few years."

"Every few years?" Charlotte repeated softly, her voice barely above a whisper. She swallowed hard, trying to push the sudden lump in her throat down, but it stubbornly refused to budge. A single tear escaped her eye, trailing down her cheek before nestling into the delicate fabric of her blouse.

"Y-yes, my dear," Agnes nodded, her own eyes glistening with unshed tears. She reached out a gentle hand, giving Charlotte's trembling one a reassuring squeeze. "It's not something I thought you knew, or else I would have said something sooner."

The warmth of Agnes's touch did little to quell the whirlwind of emotions churning within Charlotte. Her thoughts raced, swirling like autumn leaves caught in a gust of wind, as she tried to comprehend the truth about her father's visits to the quaint seaside town. As an artist, she had found solace in the beauty of Chesham Cove, and now it seemed that her father shared that connection too. But why?

"Agnes," Charlotte began, her voice cracking under the strain of suppressed sobs. "Why didn't he ever tell me? Why didn't he ever reach out to us?"

"Charlotte, my dear, I wish I had the answers you seek," Agnes replied softly, her eyes filled with genuine concern for her niece's anguish. "But I don't know what goes on in your father's heart. All I can tell you is that he comes here, to this place you both love, and maybe... Maybe there's still a chance for you to reconnect with him."

The thought of rebuilding the lost bond between herself and her father seemed like a distant dream, a hazy mirage shimmering on the horizon. Yet, as Agnes's words settled into her heart, Charlotte felt the first flicker of hope ignite within her—a tiny flame, daring to defy the darkness that threatened to engulf her.

The warm glow of the fireplace danced in Charlotte's eyes, casting shadows that seemed to play out the turmoil within her. She clutched her teacup, her knuckles white from holding it so tightly, as she tried to make sense of Agnes's revelation. The delicate china rattled against its saucer with every tremble, mimicking the disarray of Charlotte's thoughts.

"Agnes," Charlotte whispered, her words barely audible over the crackling fire. "Why would he come here and not tell me? What could possibly keep him away from me and Roxanne after all these years?"

Agnes leaned forward, the sympathy in her gaze palpable as she reached out a hand to touch Charlotte's trembling fingers. "Charlotte, I cannot pretend to know the reasons for your father's actions," she said gently. "All I know is that Henry loves Chesham Cove just as much as you do. His visits here don't diminish the bond you once shared, nor do they reflect on your worth."

"Then *why...?*" Charlotte trailed off, her voice breaking under the weight of her unspoken questions. A single tear escaped from the corner of her eye, tracing a glistening path down her cheek.

"Sometimes, people need time to heal and find their way back to those they love," Agnes replied, offering a reassuring smile. "Perhaps your father needed this time to confront his own demons before he could face you again. Losing your mother, it did something to him."

Charlotte looked down into her tea, the swirling liquid mirroring the storm of emotions brewing inside her. Could it be true? Did her father carry his own burdens, locked away behind the walls of silence that had grown between them?

"Maybe you're right, Agnes," Charlotte murmured, more to herself than to her aunt. She took a deep breath, allowing the fragrant steam from her tea to envelop her senses and ground her amidst the chaos in her mind. "I just wish I knew for sure."

"Give it time, Charlotte," Agnes said softly, squeezing her niece's hand. "The answers you seek may yet come to light."

A wave of melancholy washed over Charlotte as she considered the years that had slipped away like sand through an hourglass, each grain representing a moment she could have shared with her father. Her heart ached at the thought of the countless memories never made, the laughter they never shared, and the conversations left unspoken.

A soft breeze drifted through the open window, carrying the scent of salty sea air. The distant sound of seagulls cawing overhead tugged at Charlotte's heartstrings, as if beckoning her to return to the place where her fondest childhood memories had been made.

Charlotte's thoughts drifted to the sun-drenched days spent exploring the rugged coastline with her father by her side. She closed her eyes, recalling how the wind had whipped through her hair as they climbed rocky outcrops and discovered hidden coves together. Those moments, frozen in time, had once seemed so simple and yet so infinitely precious.

"Family is important, Charlotte," Agnes continued, her voice soft but resolute. "And I truly believe that the love between a parent and a child can never truly be lost. It may lie dormant, buried beneath layers of hurt and misunderstanding, but it's always there, waiting to be uncovered."

100

Charlotte opened her eyes and looked at Agnes, feeling the weight of her words settling deep within her soul. She knew that her cousin was right. There was still time to mend the broken threads that connected her to her father. A glimmer of hope flickered in Charlotte's eyes as she absorbed Agnes's words. While it wasn't the reunion she had envisioned, the knowledge that her father was still present in some capacity brought a sense of comfort she hadn't realized she needed.

"Thank you for telling me the truth about his visits," Charlotte whispered, feeling a mixture of relief and apprehension wash over her. "It means more than you know."

"Family is important, Charlotte," Agnes replied, her voice steady and kind. "Though the ties that bind us may be stretched and strained, they are not so easily broken."

Agnes gazed thoughtfully out the window for a moment before turning back to Charlotte, her expression softened by recollection.

"Last time I saw Henry was about two years ago," Agnes began, her voice carrying a distant quality as she delved into her memory. "He came to Chesham Cove unexpectedly, much like you did, I suspect."

Charlotte leaned forward in her seat, her eyes wide with curiosity, urging Agnes to continue.

"I remember it clearly," Agnes continued, her gaze turning inward. "I had just returned home from the market when I spotted him standing near the old oak tree by the creek, lost in thought. He appeared weary, as though he had been traveling for quite some time."

"Did you speak to him?" Charlotte asked, her voice barely above a whisper, as if afraid to break the fragile thread of the story.

"Yes, we spoke," Agnes confirmed, her eyes returning to Charlotte's. "It was a brief conversation, but it carried the weight of years' worth of unspoken words and emotions."

A surge of longing swept through Charlotte, her chest tightening at the thought of standing face-to-face with the father she had been estranged from for so many years. She could almost see him there, beneath the old oak tree, his shoulders weighed down by life's burdens.

"What did he say?" Charlotte pressed, hungering for every detail.

"Much of our conversation revolved around your sister, Roxanne," Agnes admitted, her words careful and measured. "She had recently been awarded something—for her job? Anyway, it made some news outfit he watched, and it made him regret not being there."

"Did he mention me at all?" Charlotte inquired, her voice tinged with hope and apprehension.

A sympathetic smile crossed Agnes's face as she reached out to gently squeeze Charlotte's hand. "He did, my dear. He asked about you, too, wondering how your art was coming along and if you were happy. There was a sadness in his eyes when he spoke of you, Charlotte—a longing for the connection that had been lost. Of course, I couldn't answer him, not having met you, but it was all rhetorical. I think he just comes here to unburden himself."

Tears welled up in Charlotte's eyes, her heart swelling with a mix of sorrow and relief. To know that her father still thought of her, despite the chasm that had formed between them, brought some solace to her aching soul.

"Thank you, Agnes," Charlotte murmured, her emotions threatening to spill over. "Thank you for sharing this with me."

"Of course, my dear," Agnes reassured her, offering a warm, understanding smile. "We're family, after all."

"Charlotte," Agnes spoke softly, drawing her attention back to the present moment. "I know you must have so many questions, and I wish I could answer them all. But what I can tell you is that Henry's visits here are sporadic, yet they always seem to carry some significance."

"Significance?" Charlotte asked, her voice barely audible as she clung to every morsel of information about her father.

"Indeed," Agnes nodded, her eyes distant as if reliving each encounter with Henry. "He never comes without reason, even if it's just to walk along the cliffs and gaze out at the sea. I believe Chesham Cove holds a special place in his heart—it's like a sanctuary for him."

Hearing this stirred something deep within Charlotte. She had felt the same about this place. As the weight of her sorrow settled on her shoulders, she took a deep breath, gathering the courage to voice her thoughts.

"Agnes, I need to find him," she declared, her voice trembling. "I want to reconnect with my father."

Her words hung heavy in the air, laden with the emotions that had been suppressed for so long. Agnes studied Charlotte's face.

"Charlotte," Agnes said quietly, her voice laced with empathy. "I understand your longing, and I wish you all the best in your search for him. I'll help you in any way I can," she said sincerely.

"Thank you," Charlotte replied, feeling a sense of relief wash over her. Although the journey ahead seemed daunting, knowing she had Agnes by her side gave her the strength to press forward. "I can't tell you how much it means to me to finally have a link to my father's side of the family."

Agnes reached across the table, her hand brushing against Charlotte's as she poured another cup of steaming tea. "Family is what you make of it," she mused, her gaze drifting toward the window as if lost in thought. "It doesn't matter how far apart we may be or how long it's been since we've seen each other. Your father"—she hesitated for a moment, choosing her words carefully— "he would be so proud to see the woman you've become, Charlotte. And I know he'll cherish the day when he can finally hold you in his arms again."

Charlotte swallowed hard, her chest tightening.

"Before you leave," Agnes said, her voice filled with warmth and affection, "I'd like to give you something."

She stood up and walked over to a small wooden cabinet, carefully removing a delicate porcelain teacup from its shelf. It was adorned with intricate hand-painted flowers, their vibrant hues shimmering in the fading light.

"Your grandmother"—Agnes paused, her eyes gleaming with emotion—"your father's mother, she loved this teacup dearly. I want you to have it. Every British girl needs a favorite teacup. "

Charlotte took the teacup from Agnes's outstretched hands, her fingers tracing the fragile contours of the porcelain.

"Promise me," Agnes implored, her voice thick with emotion, "that you'll come back soon. There's so much more I want to share with you."

"I promise," Charlotte vowed. But their time was running out—Charlotte had to make the drive back in time to meet Simon.

Charlotte stood up, the delicate teacup cradled in her hands. The fading sunlight streamed through the window, painting the cozy living room with a warm golden hue. Her heart was a whirlwind of emotions – gratitude for Agnes's warmth and openness, determination to uncover the truth about her father, and hope for the future.

Agnes reached out and squeezed Charlotte's arm gently. "Remember, you are always welcome here."

Charlotte leaned in for a heartfelt embrace with Agnes. As they pulled away, Charlotte clutched the teacup tighter, a tangible reminder of her connection to her father's family. As she stepped outside, Charlotte's mind raced with thoughts of her father, Henry, and the mysterious life he had led away from her. She felt an ache in her chest, a longing to understand and reconnect with the man who had been absent from her life for so long. She had hope that the chasm between them could be bridged.

As she walked toward her car, the gravel crunching beneath her feet, Charlotte allowed herself to imagine what that reunion might look like. Would he recognize her after all these years? Could they find a way to forge a new relationship built on trust and understanding? Or would his absence always be a wedge?

"Time will tell," she whispered to herself, the words lost in the gentle breeze that rustled through the trees. For now, she knew that she had taken a crucial first step.

With a deep breath, Charlotte climbed into her car, the teacup securely nestled on the passenger seat beside her. As she turned the key in the ignition and drove away, Charlotte knew that she was not just leaving behind a rediscovered family member, but also the first dangling thread that just might begin to unravel the knot that had bound her heart for so many years.

CHAPTER TWENTY ONE

The scenic coastal road stretched out before her, a seemingly never-ending ribbon of asphalt that twisted and turned through the picturesque countryside. Much like the road, Charlotte's thoughts veered between anticipation and trepidation, weaving through her memories of Chesham Cove and the father she'd lost.

Though she pressed down on the gas pedal and set off down the winding road, Charlotte found herself driving slower than usual, as though her reluctance to return to Chesham Cove had seeped into the very fibers of her being. The rustle of leaves swirling in the wind accompanied her journey, while the sea's salty tang filled her nostrils. Occasionally, the sun would break through the clouds, casting dappled patterns of light and shadow across the road. Each sensory detail seemed to underscore the bittersweet nature of her return – the beauty of the surroundings juxtaposed against the turmoil within her heart.

Charlotte's mind raced as she drove, replaying Agnes's words over and over again. Why hadn't her father reached out? What could possibly have kept him away all those years? And, more importantly, could she really find it within herself to forgive him?

"Stop it," she chided herself, shaking her head as if to dispel the doubts clouding her thoughts. "One step at a time."

As she neared Chesham Cove, Charlotte felt a strange sense of déjà vu wash over her. The twists and turns of the coastal road seemed to mirror the emotional rollercoaster she'd been riding since Agnes had revealed the truth about her father's visits.

The village itself appeared unchanged, despite her own new knowledge. The quaint cottages with their colorful gardens, the charming little shops, and the familiar lighthouse standing sentinel on the cliff – all of it seemed like a vivid dream, almost too perfect to be real. But as Charlotte pulled up outside the inn, as she climbed out of the car, as she rested her hand on the doorknob once more, feeling its cool brass against her skin, she gathered her courage. Her heart ached with the missed opportunities and years lost, but the prospect of rebuilding her bond with Henry – of finally understanding him – was too tantalizing to ignore.

If only she could find him. Or he could find her here in Chesham Cove.

Charlotte shook off her turmoil. She needed to get ready to meet Simon.

***

Charlotte stood in front of the full-length mirror that adorned her temporary bedroom, biting her bottom lip as she studied her reflection. Her fingers twitched nervously at the hem of the floral dress she had chosen for her date with Simon. The fabric felt foreign against her skin, like it belonged to someone else – someone bold and daring, unlike herself. The dress hugged her curves and accentuated her eyes but left her feeling exposed. She could still feel the lingering touch of Daniel's fingers on her arm as he'd helped her into it years ago. Would Simon find her attractive in this? Would he even notice?

"Get a grip, Charlotte," she whispered to her reflection, trying to force a smile. "It's just dinner."

But she knew it wasn't just dinner. It was a step forward or backward, depending on how she looked at it. This was her opportunity to explore her feelings for Simon, to see if there was a future beyond their shared past. And yet, doubt gnawed at her insides. Was she doing this for the right reasons? Was she truly ready to let go of Daniel's memory and allow herself to love again? She felt a knot forming in the pit of her stomach – this was her first second date in years, and the prospect of making a good impression weighed heavily on her mind. Especially since her kiss goof.

"Maybe this is too much," she mumbled to herself, pulling at the fabric. The dress seemed too bright, too attention-grabbing for an evening spent in the cozy confines of Chesham Cove's only pub. With a sigh, she stepped out of the dress and tossed it onto the growing pile of discarded clothing on the bed.

Her eyes scanned her limited wardrobe, each piece of clothing seeming to taunt her with its inadequacy. As she picked up a simple white blouse and a pair of jeans, Charlotte's thoughts drifted to her estranged husband, Daniel. He always had an opinion on what she should wear, how she should look, and even though he was thousands of miles away, his voice still echoed in the back of her mind. But this time, she was determined to silence it.

"Okay, let's try this again," she whispered, slipping into the blouse and jeans. They fit comfortably, hugging her curves without feeling restrictive. Yet, as she looked in the mirror, she couldn't shake the feeling that it wasn't enough – that she wasn't enough.

Simon is so...effortlessly charming, Charlotte thought. *And I'm just...me.*

She tried on another outfit, then another, but nothing felt right. The pressure of making a good impression on Simon gnawed at her, and she couldn't shake the fear that he would be disappointed with who she was behind the facade of an artist taking refuge in a small English town. Perhaps, she thought, it would be easier if she didn't care so much about what others thought.

"Maybe this one?" Charlotte asked her reflection, holding up a navy blue sweater and a flowing skirt. It was a balance between casual and dressy, but still, she hesitated. It felt like no matter what she chose to wear, she couldn't silence the self-doubt that had taken up residence in her chest – a doubt that stemmed from more than just wardrobe choices.

"Get a grip, Charlotte," she whispered as she changed into the sweater and skirt, hoping that by some miracle, this combination would ease her anxiety. But as she looked in the mirror once more, her heart sank – she knew that no outfit could soothe the storm of emotions brewing within her.

Charlotte's fingers ran along the hangers, her eyes flitting between a casual blouse and a more elegant dress. She could imagine Simon in his rugged attire, comfortable in his own skin as they strolled along the shoreline. Would he appreciate the effort she'd put into dressing up? Or would it make her seem out of place?

"Maybe...this one?" she mused aloud, holding up the blouse to her chest. It was simple yet stylish – perhaps an appropriate choice for their date. But as she glanced down at the dress, she couldn't help but feel drawn to its elegance.

"Ugh, why is this so hard?" Charlotte sighed, setting the blouse back on the rack. She knew that her indecisiveness wasn't solely about clothing – it was a symptom of her deep-rooted people-pleasing tendencies. And now, more than ever, she wanted to make the right impression on Simon and fit in with the locals.

As she debated her outfit options, a sudden ringing broke through her thoughts. Her phone lit up with Daniel's name, and her stomach clenched with anxiety. She hesitated, unsure whether to answer or let it go to voicemail. But the familiar pull of pleasing others won out, and she reluctantly pressed the green button.

"Hello?" she said tentatively, her voice betraying her unease.

"Charlotte," Daniel's clipped tone came through the speaker, sending shivers down her spine. "We need to talk."

"Daniel, I'm kind of busy right now," she replied, attempting to regain control of the conversation. The thought of dealing with him while also stressing over her date with Simon felt overwhelming.

"Too busy for your husband?" Daniel scoffed, the edge in his voice cutting through her defenses. "It's important, Charlotte."

She closed her eyes and took a deep breath, reminding herself that she had every right to prioritize her own needs. And that he didn't want to be her husband anymore. But as she opened her mouth to tell him that, the words caught in her throat – old habits were hard to break.

"Fine," she said, her voice wavering. "What's so important? I'm visiting Chesham Cove for a while, so there's a big time difference. It's getting late here."

It was just a little white lie.

As Daniel began to speak, Charlotte glanced back at the mirror, torn between two worlds. One where she would continue to cater to others' desires and one where she could finally live for herself. And as her husband's demands echoed through the phone, she knew that only one could lead to true happiness.

"Wait, you're in England?" Daniel's voice was full of shock and disbelief. "What the hell are you doing there, Charlotte? We have unfinished business here, and you just up and leave?"

The surprise in his tone made her wince. She should have known that he would find out sooner or later, but she hadn't expected it to be this soon. As much as she wanted to assert herself and tell him that she needed a fresh start, she couldn't bring herself to do so.

"Daniel, I... I'm sorry," she stammered, her heart pounding in her chest. "I just needed some time to think, to figure things out."

"Figure things out?" He scoffed. "This is not the time for you to run away on some wild adventure. We need to finalize our divorce, Charlotte."

The mention of their impending divorce sent a wave of conflicting emotions through her. Though she knew that their marriage had been crumbling for years, the finality of it all still left her feeling vulnerable and lost. But at the same time, her experiences in England – the people she'd met, the new joy she'd discovered – filled her with a sense of hope and excitement that she hadn't felt in a long time.

"Daniel, I know we need to deal with the divorce, but I also need to deal with myself," Charlotte said, her voice barely more than a whisper. "I can't keep living my life for everyone else. I need to find who I am again."

"Who you are?" Daniel's voice was cold and unyielding. "You're my wife, Charlotte. And as your husband, I expect you to come home and take care of what needs to be done."

Charlotte looked down at her hands, clenched together in her lap. She could feel the weight of her old life bearing down on her, the pressure to conform and please others threatening to crush her newfound dreams. She thought of Simon and the kindness he'd shown her, the way his eyes had lit up when they talked about art and books. Could she really give all that up to return to a life that had left her so unfulfilled?

"Daniel," she began, her voice trembling with the effort to stand her ground, "I need this time for myself. I promise I'll come back when I'm ready, but for now, please –" Her voice broke, tears welling up in her eyes. "Please let me have this."

There was a tense silence on the other end of the line, and Charlotte held her breath, waiting for Daniel's response. But as the seconds ticked by, I wondered if she was making a terrible mistake.

Charlotte's fingers tightened around the phone, her heart pounding in her ears as she considered the weight of Daniel's words. The warm sunlight streaming through the window cast a golden glow on the room, but it did little to alleviate the chill that had settled over her spirit.

"Daniel," she whispered, feeling the pressure of his demands and the crushing weight of her own doubts, "I can't just drop everything and come home. I need to know who I am outside of our life together. You said it yourself."

His silence unnerved her, making her question the path she had chosen. It was true, she'd been impulsive in coming to England, but the thrill of adventure and self-discovery had been irresistible. Was it really so wrong to chase after her own happiness for once?

"Charlotte," Daniel said, his voice cold and measured, "you have responsibilities at home. You can't just run away from them."

She closed her eyes, picturing their life together – the house filled with expensive furniture, the endless dinner parties with friends that he was close with, but she barely knew, and the growing chasm between them that seemed impossible to bridge. A tear slid down her cheek as she struggled to find the words to express the depth of her longing for something more.

"Daniel, I'm not running away," she finally managed, her voice wavering. "I'm trying to find myself again. To remember what it's like to be passionate, to explore the world without fear or limitation. I need this, just like you said. We both deserve better, remember? Both of us."

"Both of us?" he scoffed. "How does you abandoning me benefit our relationship?"

"Daniel," she said softly, her heart heavy with the knowledge of the truth that had remained unspoken for too long, "we don't have a relationship. You depended on me for years and then raked me over the coals for it. That's not love. I'm staying here."

There was another pause, and Charlotte held her breath, waiting for his response. She knew that her decision to stay in England was selfish in some ways, but she couldn't deny the happiness that had been rekindled within her since arriving in this quaint village.

"Fine," Daniel finally said, his voice icy. "Stay in England. All this can be done over email."

The line went dead, and Charlotte slowly lowered the phone from her ear, her heart aching with the knowledge that her pursuit of happiness might cost her everything she once held dear. Charlotte's hand trembled as she clutched the phone to her chest. The room seemed to spin around her, leaving her feeling disoriented and unsure of herself.

Had she made the right choice in staying? Or was she simply prolonging the inevitable, dragging out the pain of their separation by refusing to confront it head-on?

Lost in her thoughts, she didn't notice the doorbell ringing until it echoed through the house a second time. Her heart skipped a beat as she remembered her upcoming date with Simon, and suddenly, the weight of her decision felt heavier than ever before.

Charlotte's mind was a whirlwind of conflicting thoughts and emotions. She stared at her reflection in the mirror, her eyes glassy with unshed tears. The uncertainty she felt was palpable, like a cold hand gripping her heart.

"Pull yourself together, Charlotte," she whispered to herself. Her voice sounded distant, as if it belonged to someone else entirely. It was getting harder and harder to recognize the woman staring back at her.

"Coming!" she called out, forcing a brightness into her voice that didn't match the turmoil inside. As she made her way down the flights of stairs to the front door, she couldn't escape the nagging feeling that whatever happened tonight would have a lasting impact on her decision-making process.

Simon stood in the living room, flowers in hand, dressed in a crisp white shirt and dark slacks that made him look effortlessly handsome. As he caught sight of Charlotte, his eyes widened in admiration.

"Wow, you look stunning," he said, handing her the bouquet.

"Thank you," she replied, a blush creeping up her cheeks. "You look great too."

"Shall we?" He offered her his arm, which she hesitantly accepted, and they walked out into the evening air. The weight of her conversation with Daniel still pressed heavily on her shoulders.

"Is everything alright?" Simon asked, concern furrowing his brow as he studied her face.

"Of course," she lied, her voice wavering ever so slightly. "I'm just... really looking forward to tonight."

"Me too," he replied, offering a reassuring smile that seemed to say everything would be fine. But as they walked hand in hand toward the quaint little bistro where their date awaited, Charlotte couldn't help but question her own sanity and the path she'd chosen.

As the sun began to set, casting a golden glow over the village, Charlotte wondered if the choices she made tonight would bring her closer to happiness or push her further away from it.

CHAPTER TWENTY TWO

As they strolled toward the restaurant, Charlotte mulled over the sense of dissonance between her outward appearance and her inner turmoil. Her emotions were a tangled mess, like the wildflowers of Chesham Cove that twisted and turned in the salty breeze. She wanted to be happy, to allow herself the chance to feel something other than grief and loss. But could she truly give her heart to Simon without betraying Daniel's memory?

"Are you sure you're okay?" Simon asked, his brow furrowed with concern.

"Of course," Charlotte lied, forcing a smile. "Just a little nervous, I suppose."

"Nothing to be nervous about," he reassured her, giving her hand a gentle squeeze.

But there was everything to be nervous about, she thought. What if she couldn't move forward? What if she wasn't ready to let go? As they approached the restaurant, Charlotte felt the weight of her decision pressing down on her. Pursuing a relationship with Simon, or letting him go – she knew that whatever choice she made, it would change her life forever.

As Charlotte and Simon took their seats at the small table by the window, the flickering candlelight cast warm, golden shadows on the white linen tablecloth. The soft murmur of conversations mingled with the clinking of silverware, creating a cozy atmosphere within the intimate restaurant.

"Thank you for bringing me here," Charlotte said quietly, her eyes sweeping over the menu. "The place is lovely."

"Of course," Simon replied, his easygoing smile reaching his eyes. "I thought it was time we had a proper date. We deserve a nice evening out."

Charlotte forced a smile and nodded, but her thoughts were elsewhere. She couldn't shake the feeling that she was betraying Daniel by being here with another man.

But Daniel is divorcing you!

Her heart ached with uncertainty, and she found herself unable to fully engage in the conversation with Simon. Instead, she absently fiddled with the silverware, her focus drifting from the words on the menu to the delicate wine glasses resting on the edge of the table.

Simon noticed her distant demeanor and reached across the table, placing his hand gently over hers. "Hey," he murmured, his voice tinged with concern. "You don't have to pretend everything's fine if it's not. I'm here for you, Charlotte."

She looked up, her eyes meeting his, and saw the understanding in his gaze. It was comforting to know that he didn't expect her to be perfect, that he was willing to be patient with her as she navigated this new chapter of her life. But it also made her feel even more conflicted about her feelings for him.

"Thank you, Simon," she whispered, offering him a weak smile. "I just... I'm struggling, and I can't help but wonder if I'm making the right choices."

"Only you can answer that," he replied softly. "But you want to talk about it?"

"Not now," she said. "Let's just enjoy our meal."

As they shared a meal, the tension between them slowly began to dissipate. Charlotte found herself more at ease with Simon's presence and his understanding nature. But beneath the surface, her uncertainty still lingered, casting a shadow over the dinner.

"Would you like some dessert?" Simon asked after they had finished their main courses.

"Actually, I think I could use some fresh air," Charlotte suggested, needing a moment alone to collect her thoughts.

"Of course," Simon agreed, his easygoing demeanor unwavering. "Let's take a walk down to the shore. It's beautiful at night."

The two walked hand in hand, the cool breeze carrying the scent of the sea as they strolled along the moonlit beach. Simon's patience and understanding gave Charlotte the space she needed to process her emotions, but it did little to dispel the turmoil within her heart.

The rhythmic sound of the waves crashing against the shore provided a soothing backdrop as Charlotte and Simon walked side by side. The salty sea breeze tugged at her hair, freeing strands from her carefully arranged updo, but she found that she didn't care. She was grateful for the peaceful moment, a brief reprieve from the storm of emotions raging inside her.

"Charlotte," Simon began, breaking the silence, "Please talk to me."

His voice was gentle, full of genuine concern, and it tugged at something deep within her. For so long, she had kept her feelings bottled up inside, and the thought of finally confiding in someone both terrified and relieved her.

"Simon," she hesitated, her gaze fixed on the dark water, "I'm just... overwhelmed. I've spent my entire life trying to please others, especially Daniel. And now, with everything that's happened, I'm not sure who I am anymore or what I want."

As the words spilled out, Charlotte felt a weight lifted off her chest. Simon squeezed her hand reassuringly, his strong fingers warm and steady against her skin.

"Charlotte, it's okay to feel lost," he told her softly. "But you need to take some time to figure out what you truly want in life. Not what Daniel wants, or anyone else, but what makes you happy."

His words resonated within her, forcing Charlotte to confront the conflict that had been brewing beneath the surface. For years, she had sought validation from those around her, eager to fulfill their expectations and mold herself into the person they wanted her to be. But now, with her world turned upside down, she questioned if that was the right path for her.

"Is it selfish to want something different?" she asked, uncertainty creeping into her voice.

"Absolutely not," Simon replied emphatically. "You have every right to prioritize your own happiness and well-being. And if that means making a change, then so be it."

Charlotte chewed on her lip, mulling over his words as they continued their walk. The idea of making decisions for herself, without seeking the approval of others, was both exhilarating and daunting. But wasn't that what she had always wanted – the freedom to choose her own path, to explore her passions and desires without judgment?

"I have a lot to think about," she whispered, her voice barely audible above the sound of the waves.

He nodded, his eyes reflecting the moonlight as he turned to face her. And then, he simply held out his hand. Under the glow of the silver moon, Charlotte and Simon ambled along the shoreline, their footprints trailing behind them in the damp sand. The salty sea breeze ruffled her hair, sending tendrils tickling across her cheeks. As they reached a stretch of beach illuminated by moonlight, Simon hesitated, his hand lingering on her arm.

"Charlotte," he began, his voice strained with emotion. "I can't help but feel this undeniable connection between us, and I hope you feel it too."

Her heart pounded against her ribcage, echoing the rhythm of the waves crashing onto the shore. She knew what he was saying was true – there was an undeniable spark between them, but she couldn't ignore the nagging doubts that plagued her mind.

"Simon, I..." she trailed off, her eyes darting away from his intense gaze, searching for some semblance of clarity within the shadows cast by the towering cliffs.

"May I?" he asked softly, his warm breath caressing her cheek as he leaned closer. His brown eyes, darkened further by the night, searched her face for permission.

As his lips brushed against hers, a tidal wave of emotions overwhelmed her. The taste of salt mingled with the faint scent of his aftershave, creating an intoxicating cocktail that left her breathless. But amidst the passion, her thoughts raced with confusion and hesitation, and she gently placed her hands on his chest, pushing him away.

"Simon, I'm sorry," she whispered, her voice quivering as she averted her gaze. "It's just... everything is happening so fast, and I don't know if I'm ready for this."

He regarded her with a tender smile, his eyes softening with understanding. "Charlotte, it's okay," he reassured her, his thumb lightly grazing her cheek. "I don't want to rush you into anything you're not ready for. We can take things slow, as slow as you need."

"Thank you," she breathed. "I just... I need some time to figure out what I truly want."

"Take all the time you need," he said gently, his hand slipping from her arm as they resumed their walk along the shoreline. As they moved through the moonlit night, Charlotte's thoughts swirled. And as the waves continued to kiss the shore, she wondered if one day, she would be able to surrender herself completely to the uncharted waters of love.

The salty sea breeze caressed Charlotte's cheeks as she stared out at the inky expanse of water. She shivered involuntarily, feeling both exposed and vulnerable under the watchful eye of the moon. Simon walked beside her, his steady presence a quiet comfort as they moved further from the shore.

"Can I ask you something?" he ventured hesitantly, breaking the silence that had settled between them like a thick fog.

"Of course," she replied.

"Have you ever really allowed yourself to make choices based on what you truly want, rather than what others expect of you?"

Her heart quickened as she considered his words, her thoughts tumbling like stones caught in a relentless current. The truth was, she couldn't recall a time when she had made a decision solely for herself, without seeking validation or approval from others.

"I... I don't know," she admitted, the vulnerability in her voice betraying the depth of her struggle. "I've always been so focused on fulfilling the expectations of those around me – my family, my friends, even my husband."

Simon nodded thoughtfully, his brow furrowed with concern. "There's nothing wrong with wanting to make others happy, but sometimes it's important to look inward and consider our own needs and desires. It's an essential part of self-discovery and growth."

"Self-discovery..." she mused, tasting the unfamiliarity of the word on her tongue. "I suppose I haven't given myself the opportunity to truly explore who I am or what I want."

The lights of the inn grew nearer, casting a warm glow upon their faces as they approached. Simon's voice broke through her thoughts, his concern etched across his rugged features. "You've gone quiet again. Is everything alright?"

She glanced at him, taking solace in the warmth of his eyes. "I'm just... trying to process everything," she admitted, her hands wringing together. "It's not easy, realizing I've spent most of my adult life seeking validation from others."

"Learning to trust yourself can be difficult," Simon acknowledged, placing a comforting hand on her shoulder. "Even for mermaids."

"Small steps..." she said, chuckling a little under her breath, attempting to grasp onto the concept. A part of her longed for the simplicity of her previous life, where she relied on others to make choices for her. But another part yearned for the freedom and autonomy she had been denying herself for so long. It was this internal struggle that made her heart race, her palms sweat, her breath come in shallow gasps.

"Like choosing what to paint next," Simon suggested gently, his eyes searching hers for understanding. "You do that all the time, right? Or deciding which path to take on a walk. Start with the simple things, and eventually, you'll build up the courage to tackle the bigger decisions."

As they ascended the creaking staircase, Charlotte couldn't shake the sensation of standing at a precipice, the vast unknown stretching out before her. Every step she took felt both exhilarating and terrifying, as if she were venturing into uncharted territory. As she reached the front door, she paused, turning back toward Simon.

"Goodnight, Simon," she said hesitantly, her voice wavering with apprehension.

"Goodnight, Charlotte," he replied with a reassuring smile. "And I look forward to date number three."

CHAPTER TWENTY THREE

Charlotte bolted upright in bed, her heart pounding and her breath coming in short, heavy gasps. Sweat beaded on her forehead, and her hands trembled as she attempted to steady herself. The nightmare had been so vivid, a tangled web of painful memories and haunting images that seemed hell-bent on tormenting her.

She lay back down, pulling the covers up to her chin, as if the thin cotton could shield her from the lingering emotions of her dream. Her chest heaved, struggling to catch her breath as the terror slowly ebbed away, only to be replaced by an unsettling sense of unease.

"Deep breaths, Charlotte," she whispered to herself, trying to shake off the remnants of her nightmare. "It's just a dream."

But as she stared at the ceiling in the dark room, listening to the soft rustle of the leaves outside her window, she couldn't deny the overwhelming sense of dread that tightened its grip on her heart. She should have rested peacefully after spending such a lovely time with Simon, but instead her mind had conjured the jeering faces from the art gallery back in New York and Daniel, his own face full of distaste as he ran down every weakness and fault she had. The dream had dredged up fears and insecurities that she had spent years trying to suppress, and now they threatened to consume her.

"Get a grip, Charlotte," she chided herself, her voice barely audible.

But in the quiet stillness of the night, with only the shadows for company, Charlotte wondered if that were true.

As the darkness of the room pressed in on her, Charlotte's thoughts began to race. Nightmares were one thing, but deep down, she knew her subconscious was trying to tell her something. These weren't just random fears or anxieties; they were a manifestation of all the unresolved issues she had been avoiding for far too long.

"Enough," she whispered resolutely, sitting up in bed. She couldn't let herself be paralyzed by fear any longer.

"Daniel deserves better?" she laughed and mused aloud, thinking of her husband and their strained relationship. "And so do I. So I'll give him his divorce..."

With newfound courage, Charlotte reached for her phone, her fingers trembling slightly as she navigated to the airline's website. Each tap of her finger felt like an affirmation – she would return home and confront the challenges that had been looming over her for years. It wasn't going to be easy, but she needed to take control of her life, no matter how frightening it seemed at first.

"Come on, Charlotte," she murmured, her voice wavering with a mix of hope and anxiety. "You can do this."

As she scrolled through the available flights, her stomach twisted into knots. But she refused to back down, her actions fueled by the knowledge that only she could make the changes necessary for a happier, more fulfilling life.

"Let's just pick a date and go," she whispered, taking a deep breath before finally selecting a flight that would take her back home in just a few days. This decision, though terrifying, felt oddly liberating. For the first time in what felt like forever, Charlotte was taking charge of her own destiny.

Charlotte's finger hovered above the "Confirm" button, her heart pounding in her chest. But before she could press it, an error message appeared on her phone screen, indicating that there was no cell service. She stared at the screen, a wave of frustration and disappointment washing over her, making her feel trapped in her current situation.

"Of course," she muttered, shaking her head in disbelief. The one time she mustered up the courage to face her problems head-on, and she couldn't even book a flight to do so. It seemed as though the universe was conspiring against her, forcing her to remain stuck at Chesham Cove.

"Maybe it's a sign," she whispered to herself. "Maybe I need more time to think."

"Or maybe you just need to get out of this room for a bit," she reasoned, glancing around the small space that had become her temporary home. Charlotte decided that a walk along the beach would help clear her mind and gather her thoughts, providing some much-needed clarity amid the chaos.

"Alright," she murmured, slipping on a pair of sandals. "If you can't fly home right now, you might as well make the most of this place."

As she stepped out onto the soft sand, Charlotte allowed her thoughts to wander. The serenity of the beach enveloped her, inviting her to contemplate the decisions that had led her to this moment. With each step, she weighed the pros and cons of staying versus going, trying to determine what path would bring her true happiness.

As Charlotte walked further from the inn, she periodically checked her phone for cell service. Each time it failed to connect, she felt a pang of frustration – but also a strange sense of relief, as if being forced to stay in Chesham Cove allowed her to delay the inevitable confrontation with her past.

The rhythmic sound of the crashing waves called to Charlotte as she stepped onto the beach, her feet sinking into the damp sand. The ocean breeze carried the briny scent of the sea, mingling with the earthy aroma of seaweed strewn across the shoreline. With each step, the sand embraced her toes like a tender, familiar caress, grounding her in the moment.

As she walked along the shore, the frothy waves lapped at her feet, erasing her footprints as quickly as they were made. It was as if the water was trying to tell her something – that nothing was permanent, and change was inevitable.

Charlotte's thoughts drifted back to her past, reflecting on the choices she had made and the life she had built with Daniel. Her heart clenched as she tried to imagine what her future would look like without him, feeling as though her world was crumbling beneath her feet.

For years, Charlotte had craved stability and familiarity, clinging to their comforting embrace like a lifeline—so much so that she had become like furniture in her own household, to her own husband. But now, with each step she took through the soft sand, she felt an unfamiliar tug at her heart, urging her to let go of the past and embrace the boundless possibilities that lay ahead.

"Is it wrong to want something more?" she asked herself, her inner turmoil manifesting as a tight knot in her chest.

As if searching for answers, Charlotte pulled out her phone and glanced down at the screen, only to be met with the same frustrating lack of cell service that had plagued her since her arrival. She sighed, feeling momentarily trapped by her inability to simply book a plane ticket and escape the difficult decisions that awaited her.

"Maybe it's a sign," she mused, tucking her phone back into her pocket. "Perhaps I'm meant to stay here."

With every step, Charlotte felt the weight of her old life easing off her shoulders, replaced by a growing sense of adventure and possibility. The quiet beauty of Chesham Cove seemed to hold a certain magic, one that whispered of new beginnings and untapped potential.

A fresh ocean breeze brushed past Charlotte's cheeks, invigorating her senses and breathing life into her weary soul. She drew in a deep breath, allowing the salty air to fill her lungs and clear her thoughts. With each step along the shoreline, she felt a growing sense of clarity and determination. Her gaze fell upon a massive structure up ahead, its imposing presence unmistakable even from a distance. It was Thomas Windnell's luxury resort – the very one Marge had warned her about. As Charlotte approached the sprawling complex, she was struck by the stark contrast it presented against the quaint charm of Chesham Cove.

"Look at this place," she whispered, her eyes tracing the sleek lines of the modern building. "Marge was right. If Windnell keeps expanding like this, there won't be anything left of the cove."

She paused for a moment, taking in the full extent of the resort. It loomed over the pristine beach like an unwelcome intruder, casting a shadow that threatened to swallow the delicate balance of the cove's tourism trade.

Windnell doesn't care about preserving the magic of Chesham Cove, she thought bitterly. *He just wants to line his pockets and move on to the next big project.* She had met many like him through Daniel's line of work.

Charlotte closed her eyes, envisioning a future where Chesham Cove was unrecognizable – its vibrant community replaced with sterile resorts that catered only to the wealthy elite. A sense of urgency washed over her, sparking the urge to protect the cove and its people.

"Daniel would say I'm being impulsive," she mused, a small smile playing on her lips. He would have discouraged it. "But sometimes, you have to follow your instincts."

With a deep breath, she turned her back on the resort and began to retrace her steps along the beach. Her heart pounded with determination as she set off toward the inn, her steps sure and unwavering.

"Chesham Cove is worth fighting for," she vowed, her voice resolute against the crashing waves. "And I won't let Windnell – or anyone else – destroy it."

With her jaw set and a fierce glint in her eyes, Charlotte pivoted on her heel and marched back along the shoreline. The coarse sand crunched beneath her feet, echoing the newfound resolve that surged through her veins. Her steps were more purposeful now, each one leaving a lasting imprint on the beach. As she continued her trek, the salty air whipped at her face, stinging her cheeks and leaving them flushed with determination.

"Windnell can't have this place," she muttered to herself, her words carried away by the ocean breeze. "I won't let him."

CHAPTER TWENTY FOUR

Charlotte's heart pounded in her chest as she dashed back to The Crown Inn, the cobblestone streets of Chesham Cove a blur beneath her feet. A gust of cool wind blew through her hair, carrying with it the scent of sea salt and fresh bread from a nearby bakery. She knew she had made up her mind, and there was no turning back now.

Bursting through the door, Charlotte darted into the warm, inviting kitchen. Marge stood at the counter, kneading dough expertly between her fingers. Floured hands paused midair as she glanced up in surprise at the sudden intrusion.

"Charlotte, dear," she said, concern furrowing her brow. "What's gotten into you?"

"I want to buy the inn, Marge!" Charlotte blurted out, her words tumbling over each other in her excitement. Her eyes sparkled with determination, and she clasped her hands together, gripping them tight to still their trembling. "I've been thinking about it ever since I arrived, and I know this is what I'm meant to do."

Marge's mouth fell open, her normally composed demeanor faltering as she stared at the breathless woman before her. The dough in her hands slowly returned to the counter, forgotten for the moment. "You...you want to buy The Crown Inn?" she stammered, her eyes wide with shock.

"Yes, Marge! I've never been more certain of anything in my life." Charlotte's voice wavered with emotion as she imagined the possibilities, envisioning the inn turned into a charming bed and breakfast full of warmth and laughter.

Marge blinked rapidly, seemingly trying to process the unexpected request.

"Charlotte..." Marge began, her voice trailing off as she searched for the right words. She knew how much The Crown Inn meant to Marge, but perhaps it was time for a change. And if anyone could breathe new life into it, it was Charlotte herself.

Seeing the hesitation in Marge's eyes, Charlotte took a deep breath and tried to steady herself. "I know this is sudden, but I promise you, Marge, I'm serious about this," she said firmly, her gaze never leaving

123

the older woman's face. "Can we please discuss the details? I want to make this happen."

Marge hesitated for a moment longer, studying the determination etched into every line of Charlotte's face. The scent of fresh-baked bread filled the air around them, mingling with the warmth emanating from the hearth. Finally, she let out a sigh and nodded, her eyes crinkling with a small, hesitant smile.

"Alright," Marge agreed, wiping her flour-dusted hands on her apron. "Let's sit down and talk about it properly, then. You look like you could use some tea to calm those nerves of yours." She gestured to the sturdy wooden table nestled against the kitchen wall, inviting Charlotte to take a seat.

"Thank you, Marge," Charlotte murmured gratefully, settling onto the bench and smoothing her skirt beneath her. As Marge bustled about preparing the tea, Charlotte relaxed into the comforting familiarity of the scene: the way the sun filtered through the lace curtains, casting dappled shadows across the well-worn floorboards; the faint hum of bees buzzing just outside the open window; the gentle clink of china as Marge set down their teacups—one of her own, and Charlotte's new favorite family heirloom cup.

"Here you go, dear," Marge said, handing Charlotte a steaming cup of tea. The aroma was rich and fragrant, wafting up from the delicate porcelain and filling Charlotte's senses with a sense of calm. "Now, let's get down to business, shall we?"

Charlotte took a slow sip of her tea, feeling the warmth spread through her body and soothe her pounding heart. She looked into Marge's eyes, the older woman's expression open and attentive, and knew that she had found a kindred spirit in this quaint little corner of England.

"Alright," Charlotte said, setting down her cup and meeting Marge's gaze once more. "Let's talk about The Crown Inn."

"Alright, Marge," Charlotte began, her fingers drumming lightly on the table's surface. "I understand that this might be a bit sudden for you, but I need to know: how much are you asking for the inn?"

Marge hesitated, her eyes flicking around the room as if searching for an answer in the familiar surroundings. Finally, she sighed and met Charlotte's gaze. "Well, dear, I suppose I'd part with it for... oh, let's say two hundred thousand pounds."

Charlotte's heart swelled with relief, and a grin spread across her face. She had been saving up her earnings from her piecemeal art sales over the years, and while she hadn't expected an opportunity like this, she knew she could afford a significant down payment.

"Two hundred thousand," Charlotte echoed thoughtfully, the number feeling both daunting and entirely possible all at once. "I think I can manage that."

"Are you certain?" Marge asked, her brow furrowing with concern. "It's not a small sum, and I don't want you jumping into this without thinking it through."

It would wipe out her nest egg, but Charlotte was thrilled to do it.

"Believe me, Marge," Charlotte replied, her voice filled with conviction, "I've never been more sure of anything in my life. And I have... I have a vision for this place."

"Go on," Marge encouraged, leaning forward with genuine interest.

"Firstly," Charlotte said, gesturing around the cozy kitchen, "I'd like to turn The Crown Inn into a bed and breakfast. A welcoming haven for travelers and artists alike, a place where people can come to escape the chaos of their daily lives and find inspiration in the beauty of Chesham Cove."

As Charlotte spoke, her eyes filled with the dream she had begun to weave for herself – for what The Crown Inn could become. Marge listened intently, her expression softening as she took in the younger woman's enthusiasm.

"Of course, I'd want to keep the charm of the inn intact," Charlotte continued, "but perhaps with a few small updates. Fresh paint, new linens... just enough to make our guests feel at home."

"Guests?" Marge asked, a hint of a smile playing at her lips.

"Ah, yes," Charlotte laughed, a touch sheepishly. "I suppose I'm getting a bit ahead of myself. But it's hard not to when I can see it all so clearly in my mind."

"Sounds like you've given this a lot of thought," Marge noted, her eyes twinkling with approval.

"Thank you, Marge," Charlotte said sincerely, warmth filling her chest at the older woman's words. "I promise you, if you decide to sell The Crown Inn to me, I'll do everything in my power to make it a place you can be proud of."

"Something tells me, dear, that I already am."

The kitchen's familiar aroma of freshly-baked bread and brewed tea wafted over Charlotte as she watched Marge's eyes flit back and forth, her brow furrowed in contemplation. The older woman's hands were wrapped protectively around her teacup, as if drawing some measure of comfort from its warmth.

Charlotte's fingers tightened around her own cup, her heart fluttering with anticipation as she awaited the verdict.

Marge took a deep breath, her gaze steady. "Alright, my dear. I'll sell you The Crown Inn at the price we discussed. This place has been my life's work, and I can't think of anyone better to pass it on to."

"Really?" Charlotte gasped, relief and joy surging through her in equal measure. She felt the weight of her dreams begin to lift as the possibilities unfurled before her. "Oh, Marge, thank you! I promise I won't let you down."

"Something tells me you won't," Marge replied, her eyes softening as she regarded Charlotte with a mixture of admiration and affection. "Now then, let's discuss the details, shall we?"

As they delved into the particulars of the sale, Charlotte's mind raced with plans and ideas, each more exciting than the last. Through it all, however, her thoughts kept returning to one simple truth: she was finally on the path to making her dream a reality, and it filled her with a sense of purpose she hadn't known she'd been missing.

The warmth of the kitchen seemed to intensify, spreading through Charlotte's chest until she felt as if she were glowing from within. With Marge's approval secured and her dream within reach, she knew it was time to share the news with someone who had always been there for her – her sister Roxanne.

"Would you mind if I make a quick phone call?" Charlotte asked, her voice trembling with excitement.

"Of course not, dear," Marge replied, gesturing toward the telephone on the wall. "Go right ahead."

Charlotte approached the vintage rotary phone with an eagerness that belied its antiquated nature. The cold, black receiver felt heavy in her hand as she pressed it against her ear and dialed Roxanne's number from memory. The line crackled and buzzed, as if trying to keep up with the frantic pace of her heartbeat.

"Hello?" Roxanne's voice came through, laced with curiosity.

"Roxanne, it's me." Charlotte could barely contain her giddiness as she struggled to form words. "I-I did it. I'm buying The Crown Inn!"

"Wait, what?" Roxanne responded, her confusion palpable. "You're buying an inn? That old place you've been staying at?"

"Yes! Oh, Rox, you should see it. It's absolutely perfect," Charlotte gushed, her words tumbling out like water over a riverbed. "It has so much potential, and I just know that turning it into a bed and breakfast is exactly what I want to do with my life."

"Char, are you sure this isn't just a spur-of-the-moment decision?" Roxanne's initial skepticism was evident, but Charlotte could hear the trace of concern beneath it. "I mean, I want you to be happy, but this is a huge commitment."

"I know, Rox, I know," Charlotte reassured her, a fierce determination tightening her grip on the receiver. "But I've never felt more certain about anything in my life. This is what my heart has been searching for."

"Wow," Roxanne breathed, the surprise in her voice giving way to awe. "Okay, Charlotte. If you're sure about this, then I'm with you one hundred percent. We Anderson girls have always been unstoppable when we put our minds to something."

"Thank you, Rox. I love you," Charlotte replied, her eyes glistening with unshed tears of gratitude.

"Hey, what are sisters for?" Roxanne's playful tone returned as she chuckled lightly. "Now, let's hear all about this grand plan of yours."

As Charlotte eagerly recounted her vision for The Crown Inn, the comforting scent of fresh-baked bread and Marge's lavender soap enveloped her, rooting her even more firmly to this place. She knew with certainty that she belonged here.

"Rox," she said, her voice soft with determination, "I need you to do me a favor. Can you pack up my belongings and ship them to England? I'm not coming back for a while.

There was a brief pause on the other line before Roxanne responded, her tone filled with admiration. "You're really going all in, aren't you?"

"Absolutely," Charlotte replied, her eyes shining with conviction. "This is my chance to truly make a difference and build something. All on my own."

"Alright, sis, consider it done." Roxanne's voice was thick with emotion, but she quickly regained her usual sass. "Just be prepared for a few extra pairs of shoes making their way into your shipment. You know how much I love shopping."

Charlotte laughed, her heart swelling with gratitude. "Thank you, Rox."

"Of course," Roxanne reassured her, her voice gentle yet firm. "I believe in you, Charlotte. If anyone can turn that inn into something amazing, it's you."

CHAPTER TWENTY FIVE

Charlotte's fingers danced across the keys as she powered up her laptop, the familiar hum of its machinery filling the otherwise quiet room. She adjusted the camera ever so slightly, angling it upwards to capture the full essence of her beaming smile. A quick check of the internet connection reassured her that everything was in order, and with a deep breath, she clicked on Amelia's name, initiating their video call.

As the seconds ticked by, Charlotte's anticipation mounted, her heart fluttering like the wings of a hummingbird. The news she wanted to share with Amelia was too important – too life-changing – to merely send as a text or discuss over a simple phone call. She needed to see her daughter's face, to witness firsthand the excitement she knew would light up Amelia's eyes.

While she waited for the call to connect, Charlotte thought about how much her world had shifted in recent months. Gone were the days of submitting to Daniel's overbearing demands and stifling her own dreams to cater to his whims. This was her time now, her opportunity to take hold of her life and forge a new path, one filled with passion and purpose. And it all began with the enchanting little inn she'd discovered nestled in the heart of a quaint seaside town.

The sound of the call connecting snapped Charlotte back to the present, her gaze immediately drawn to the small preview window displaying her own image. She smoothed down her wavy, chestnut locks and straightened her posture, wanting to appear both poised and confident as she shared her news with Amelia. The last thing she wanted was for her daughter to sense any lingering doubts or uncertainties that might still be lurking in the corners of her mind.

The moment Amelia's face appeared on the screen, a radiant smile spread across her features, mirroring Charlotte's own. The connection between mother and daughter was undeniable – it was as if they shared a secret language all their own, one that needed no words to convey the depth of their bond.

"Hi, Mom!" Amelia beamed, her enthusiasm palpable even through the screen. "It's so good to see you! What's going on?"

"Hello, sweetheart," Charlotte replied, her heart swelling with love for her daughter. "I have some wonderful news to share with you."

"Really?" Amelia's eyes widened with curiosity. "What is it?"

"Well, I found an absolutely charming inn in this quaint seaside town. It has so much potential, Amelia. I can just picture it – cozy guest rooms filled with my paintings, a warm, inviting atmosphere where people can truly relax and feel at home..."

Amelia leaned in closer, her eyes sparkling with interest. "That sounds amazing, Mom. You're not buying it, are you? No way."

Charlotte's eyes danced as she described the inn in vivid detail. "Way. The building itself is over a century old, with beautiful wooden beams and intricate stained-glass windows. There's a lovely garden out back, perfect for afternoon teas and lazy summer evenings. And the location... Amelia, it's just steps away from the ocean. I can hear the waves crashing against the shore."

"Wow, Mom, it sounds like a dream come true," Amelia gushed, clearly captivated by her mother's vision. "I'm so happy for you. You deserve this more than anyone I know."

"Thank you, sweetie," Charlotte responded, her eyes misting with emotion. "I've been waiting so long to find something like this, and now that it's finally within reach, I can't help but feel like everything is falling into place."

"You're going to turn that inn into the most magical B&B anyone has ever seen," Amelia said, her voice filled with certainty. "And then, I'm going to be super snobby to my college friends and mention our English estate all the time."

Charlotte felt a warmth spread through her chest. This connection with her daughter – this beautiful, unbreakable bond they shared – was what truly mattered. It was the reason behind every decision she made, every step she took toward carving out a better life for herself and Amelia.

"Mom," Amelia said, her expression turning serious. "You've always been there for me, supporting me and believing in my dreams. Now, it's my turn to support you and believe in yours. I know you can make this B&B something special. You sacrificed a lot for me, growing up. It's your time now."

"Your faith in me means the world, Amelia," Charlotte whispered, tears glistening in her eyes. "I promise I won't let you down."

"Never doubted it for a second, Mom," Amelia replied, her smile returning. "Now go out there and work your artistic magic on that inn!"

Charlotte smiled back at her daughter, her heart swelling with gratitude and love.

"Watch me, sweetie," Charlotte said, her voice filled with determination.

The warmth of their conversation still lingered in the air, when Charlotte's phone suddenly rang, cutting through the cozy atmosphere like a knife. The familiar, yet unwanted ringtone sent a shiver down her spine, and she could feel her heart rate quicken as she glanced at the screen. It was Daniel.

"Mom? Who is it?" Amelia asked, concern furrowing her brow at the sight of her mother's sudden unease.

"Daniel—your dad," Charlotte replied hesitantly, her fingers hovering above the screen as she weighed her options. A part of her wanted to ignore the call, to continue basking in the love and support of her daughter, but she knew that avoiding him wouldn't solve anything. "I... I have to take this, sweetie."

"Alright, Mom," Amelia said, her voice filled with understanding. "Just remember, whatever he says, he's the jerk."

"Thank you, Amelia," Charlotte said, trying not to laugh as she reluctantly tapped the green icon to answer the call on speaker.

"Charlotte, we need to talk," Daniel's voice came through the phone, tense and curt. The sharpness of his tone rattled her nerves, but she refused to let him see how much he affected her.

"Hello, Daniel," Charlotte responded, doing her best to keep her voice steady and neutral. "What do you want?"

Daniel snapped, his irritation plain for all to hear. "I'm still waiting to know when you'll be back."

"I won't. In fact, I bought an inn. Chew on that."

His voice exploded through the phone. "Buying an old inn without even discussing it with me first? What were you thinking? "Have you lost your mind?"

"Actually, Daniel," Charlotte began, force seeping into her voice despite the lingering nervousness, "it was never your decision to make. This is my life, and I've decided to start over by turning that inn into something beautiful and welcoming."

"Charlotte, I just want what's best for you and Amelia," Daniel implored, his voice softening as though she would be swayed by feigned concern. "You don't have to prove anything to me."

"Prove?" Charlotte scoffed, her eyes blazing with indignation. "This has nothing to do with proving anything to you. This is about reclaiming my life, my dreams, and my happiness – something that was stifled during our marriage."

"Fine," Daniel sighed, his voice laden with concern, whether genuine or feigned. "But you still need to think about the financial aspect. Where will you get the funds to renovate and run this place?"

"Actually," Charlotte began, her voice strong and unwavering despite the pounding of her heart, "I've decided to sell our house. After all, it was always more mine than yours. As for the profit, I intend to keep it for myself and invest it into the inn."

"Wait just a minute!" Daniel protested, his voice sharp with disbelief. "That's our home. You can't just sell it without discussing it with me first!"

"Considering everything that's happened, Daniel, I think it's only fair that I take control of my own life and finances," Charlotte stated firmly, her voice growing stronger as she faced her estranged husband's resistance head-on. Her chest swelled with the unfamiliar feeling of empowerment, and she knew she could no longer allow him to dictate her choices.

"Charlotte," Daniel began, his voice strained as he attempted to regain control of the conversation. "You can't just—"

"Daniel, I won't be swayed by your fear or skepticism," Charlotte interrupted, her voice steady and resolute. "This is my decision, and I'm going to see it through. Now, if you'll excuse me, I need to get back to Amelia."

With that, Charlotte ended the call, her hand trembling slightly as she set the phone down on the table. She took a deep breath, allowing herself a moment of pride in standing up for herself and her dreams.

Daniel's voice continued to crackle through the phone, his words sharp and persistent. Charlotte could sense his desperation as he tried to maintain control over her choices.

"Charlotte," he pleaded, "you're making a huge mistake. You have no experience in running a business, let alone an inn. What if it doesn't work out? Have you even thought about that? Look, we can talk about this later," Daniel said, his tone suggesting he had already dismissed her words. "I'll call you tomorrow."

She picked up the phone again. "I won't answer. Goodbye, Daniel," Charlotte replied firmly, her hand shaking as she ended the call. She took a deep breath, gathering her courage like armor around her heart.

"Mom? Are you okay?" Amelia asked gently, her concern etched across her face.

"Better than ever, sweetie," Charlotte assured her daughter, her voice still wavering but filled with newfound conviction

Glancing back to the laptop screen, Charlotte met Amelia's proud smile. The knowledge of her daughter's unwavering support filled her with a fierce determination to pursue her dreams, no matter what challenges lay ahead. With every fiber of her being, Charlotte knew that this was the beginning of a new chapter—one where she would finally prioritize her own happiness and ambitions.

"Mom," Amelia said softly, her eyes shining with pride and admiration, "I'm so proud of you."

"Thank you, sweetheart," Charlotte replied, her voice thick with emotion.

It was the dawning of a new era—one of independence.

CHAPTER TWENTY SIX

The salty breeze of Chesham Cove tugged at Charlotte's chestnut curls and played with the hem of her skirt, making her feel as free and untamed as the sea before her. Her heart swelled with joy as she marveled at the beauty of her surroundings, the quaint seaside town that had welcomed her so warmly.

As she walked, her eyes scanned the bustling scene, searching for one particular individual among the fisherman, sailors, and merchants. Suddenly, there he was - Simon Harris. He stood tall and rugged, his strong hands deftly working on the ropes of a fishing boat, while his deep brown eyes seemed to reflect the very waters of the cove.

Charlotte's heart skipped a beat as excitement washed over her face, transforming her features into a picture of pure delight. There he was, the man who had stirred emotions within her she thought long buried, feelings she never imagined could resurface after all these years.

Taking in a deep breath, she felt a mix of nervousness and anticipation bubble inside her like a boiling cauldron. Her pulse raced as her mind filled with thoughts of their last encounter, the sweet stolen moments they shared, and the undeniable connection between them.

"Focus," she whispered to herself, gathering her courage. With a determined stride, she made her way toward Simon, her cheeks flushed with a mixture of excitement and nerves.

"Simon!" she called out as she drew closer, her voice a blend of warmth and eagerness.

At the sound of her voice, Simon paused in his work and looked up. A genuine smile spread across his chiseled features as he caught sight of Charlotte. "Charlotte," he replied, his tone equally excited, "I didn't expect to see you down here today."

"Neither did I," she admitted with a soft laugh, her eyes sparkling with joy. "But I found myself drawn to the harbor, and I'm so glad I did."

"Me too," Simon agreed, his gaze locked on her, as if she were the only thing that mattered in that moment. It was a rare connection, one that Charlotte felt deep in her soul and knew would change her forever.

The sea breeze tousled Charlotte's auburn hair as she approached Simon, her heart skipping a beat. The scent of salt and fish filled the air, mingling with the distant cries of seagulls overhead. Chesham Cove had always been a place of solace for Charlotte, but now, with Simon's presence, it held even more meaning.

"Simon, I wanted to tell you about my plans for The Crown," Charlotte said, her voice filled with enthusiasm and hope. "Now that I'll be the owner, I've been working on some ideas for the interior design – using reclaimed wood from old fishing boats and adding local artwork to give it a true coastal feel."

"Really?" Simon asked, his eyes brightening. "That sounds incredible, Charlotte. I love that you're embracing the history and spirit of our town. New owner, you say?" He feigned innocence. "That mean you're staying?"

With each word he spoke, Charlotte felt the warmth of genuine interest radiating from him. An unexpected sense of comfort calmed her, and she knew it was safe to share her dreams with this man who stood before her. "Yes. For quite some time."

"Well then, Charlotte," Simon began, his voice filled with excitement. "Would you allow me the pleasure of taking you on a third date?" His eyes sparkled like the sea at sunrise - full of hope and promise.

She could hardly contain her own enthusiasm as she answered, "I'd love that, Simon."

"Great," he replied with a wide, genuine smile. "I know just the place."

As they continued their conversation, the sound of heavy boots crunching on gravel caught their attention. A fisherman approached them, his weathered face creased with lines from years spent battling the elements. He waved a friendly hand as he called out, "Oi, boss! Got a minute?"

"Of course," Simon nodded to the fisherman before turning to Charlotte, his expression apologetic. "Just give me a moment, please."

As Simon stepped away to speak with the fisherman, Charlotte's mind raced with curiosity. She glanced back at Simon, admiring his strong, capable hands as he gestured while speaking to the fisherman. Boss? Could it be possible that he held a more significant role in the harbor than she had initially thought?

Lost in her thoughts, Charlotte barely noticed when Simon returned to her side. "Sorry about that," he said, his eyes warm as they met hers. "Sometimes, things need my attention around here."

"Of course," she replied, her curiosity momentarily sated by his presence. "So, where were we?"

"Ah, our next date," Simon grinned, excitement bubbling beneath his words. "I was thinking we could take a walk along the cliffs. The view is breathtaking, and I think it would be the perfect backdrop for getting to know each other even better."

"Sounds lovely," Charlotte agreed, her heart swelling with anticipation. "I can't wait."

"Neither can I," Simon admitted, his eyes full of promise as they locked onto hers. And in that moment, as the sun dipped below the horizon, painting the sky in hues of pink and gold, Charlotte felt a surge of excitement - not only for their next date but for the future unfolding before them.

"Boss?" she asked suddenly, her voice tinged with both confusion and curiosity.

"Ah, yes," Simon responded, his eyes twinkling with amusement. "I suppose I should have mentioned it before."

"Charlotte, this is Jack," he said, gesturing toward the fisherman who had joined them. The man was burly, with a salt-and-pepper beard that seemed to have seen its fair share of ocean storms. "He's one of the fishermen working under me."

"Under you?" Charlotte repeated, her eyebrows raised in surprise.

Simon chuckled, nodding as he scratched the back of his neck. "Yes, I'm actually the boss here at the harbor."

"Nice to meet you, Miss," Jack said gruffly, extending a calloused hand to Charlotte. She took it, feeling the rough texture from years of labor.

"Likewise," she replied, trying to keep the astonishment from her voice. Her gaze drifted back to Simon, taking in the rugged handsomeness that somehow seemed even more fitting given his newfound status. A sense of pride swelled within her chest, and she smiled.

"Jack, we'll discuss those issues tomorrow," Simon said, turning his attention back to the fisherman. "Right now, I'd like to spend some time with Charlotte."

"Of course, boss," Jack replied, nodding respectfully before heading back to his duties. As he disappeared into the bustling harbor, Charlotte found herself eager to learn more about this side of Simon she hadn't yet discovered.

"Quite the responsibility you have here," she said, her eyes meeting Simon's once more.

"Indeed, it keeps me on my toes," he admitted with a grin. "But I wouldn't trade it for anything." The sincerity in his voice conveyed the depth of his passion for his work, and Charlotte found herself drawn even closer to him.

Charlotte watched the fisherman walk away, his boots leaving traces in the damp sand as he rejoined the flurry of activity on the docks. Her gaze lingered for a moment before drifting back to Simon, her eyes wide with surprise and intrigue. "I had no idea you were the boss here," she admitted, her voice carrying a note of fascination.

Simon chuckled, rubbing the back of his neck. "Well, there's still a lot we don't know about each other." He gestured toward the harbor, where several boats bobbed gently in the water. "I actually own a few of these vessels. I've been working on expanding my business here in Chesham Cove."

"Wow," Charlotte breathed, her eyes following his pointing finger to the boats. The early evening sun danced upon the gentle waves, casting a warm golden glow over the scene. She could almost feel the salty breeze against her skin as she pictured Simon at the helm of one of those boats, conquering the open sea. A newfound admiration for him bubbled within her chest. "That's incredible, Simon."

"Thank you," he replied, his cheeks flushing slightly from the compliment. The wind tousled his dark hair, making him appear even more rugged and outdoorsy than usual. "It's been a challenging journey, but every time I set out on the water, I'm reminded of why I love it so much."

Charlotte was struck by the passion that shone through his words. It was clear he held a deep connection to the harbor and the community within it, something she too appreciated. In that moment, she felt a stronger bond forming between them, a shared understanding of the importance of chasing one's dreams.

"I can only imagine how rewarding it must be to see your hard work pay off."

Simon's eyes sparkled with gratitude, and he reached out to gently squeeze her hand. "It is," he agreed, his voice filled with warmth. "And I have a feeling that your inn will be just as successful." Simon's smile was contagious, and she returned it. "I've faced my fair share of obstacles, but I'm prepared to overcome them. What about your inn? Surely you have big dreams for it too?"

Charlotte nodded enthusiastically, and together, they strolled along the harbor as seagulls called overhead, their conversation flowing effortlessly between them.

"Sometimes, when I'm out there alone with nothing but the wind and the waves, I feel so free," he confessed, his eyes reflecting the depths of the sea itself. "It's like I've left all my worries behind on shore, and all that matters is that moment."

"I felt that way, painting The Crown," Charlotte murmured, her heart swelling with pride for this man she'd come to care for so deeply. "And it reminds me why I fell in love with art in the first place – the freedom to create and express myself."

"Ah, yes," Simon replied with a nod. "Art and the sea have more in common than one might think. They both offer escape."

"It seems I ran to the sea, too," she observed, and he laughed in reply. "Maybe I'm a mermaid, after all."

"Some kind of siren, to be sure," he replied.

As they made their way back to the village, Charlotte felt as though the tides were shifting – both within her heart and in the world around her. And for the first time in a long while, she was eager to embrace the change.

EPILOGUE

The early summer breeze played with Charlotte's hair as she approached The Crown Inn, her arms laden with bags from her shopping trip in town. She smiled at the sight of the quaint, ivy-covered inn that would soon be hers. A new beginning was just on the horizon.

As she stepped into the cozy lobby, she found Marge surrounded by half-filled cardboard boxes, her belongings scattered across the room like pieces of a puzzle waiting to be assembled. "Oh, Marge!" Charlotte exclaimed, her blue eyes wide with surprise. "I didn't realize you'd started packing already."

Marge looked up from her task, her round cheeks flushed from the effort. "Ah, Charlotte, my dear," she said, her voice carrying the warmth of a crackling fireplace. "Time waits for no one, and I've got so many memories to pack away."

"Let me help you," Charlotte offered, setting down her bags and rolling up the sleeves of her soft, cream-colored shirt. "It's the least I could do after all you're doing for me."

Marge smiled gratefully, her hazel eyes twinkling with kindness. "That's very sweet of you, dear." She patted a stack of newspapers beside her. "We can start with wrapping up these trinkets and baubles."

Charlotte nodded, eager to show her gratitude for the opportunity Marge was giving her. She'd always had a passion for art but never dreamed it would lead her to own an inn—a beautiful, historic one at that. As Charlotte reached for a delicate porcelain figurine, she thought of how the inn would inspire her artwork, the endless possibilities that awaited her.

"Thank you, Marge," she said earnestly, her voice catching slightly with emotion. "Owning The Crown really means the world to me."

"Of course, my dear," Marge replied gently, placing a comforting hand on Charlotte's shoulder. "I know The Crown will be in good hands."

As they continued to pack, the weight of Marge's trust settled heavily, yet warmly, on Charlotte's shoulders, like a treasured heirloom passing from one generation to another. And with it came a sense of responsibility to make The Crown Inn flourish under her care.

Charlotte glanced over at Marge, her heart swelling with gratitude and affection for the woman who had become not only her mentor but also her friend. Together, they would ensure the inn's legacy lived on, its rich history preserved and cherished for years to come.

Sunlight filtered through the lace curtains as Charlotte and Marge carefully wrapped the fragile items in layers of tissue paper. The clink of porcelain and the rustle of paper filled the room, punctuated by the soft thud of boxes being sealed shut. It was a much gentler, kinder, more hopeful process than the last pack-up she had helped with—back in New York, with Daniel.

"Would you look at this?" Marge said, holding up an intricate glass figurine of a swan. "I remember when a guest gave this to me as a thank-you gift for her wedding reception. She was such a lovely young woman."

Charlotte smiled as she imagined the scene, the inn abuzz with laughter and music, the scent of fresh flowers mingling with the warm aroma of food. As they continued packing, Marge regaled Charlotte with tales of past guests, each one seemingly more fascinating than the last.

"Ah, Mr. O'Malley," Marge reminisced, carefully placing a worn leather-bound book into a box. "He was quite the character, always spinning stories of his travels around the world. He'd sit in that very corner by the fireplace," she gestured toward the now-empty spot, "and entertain everyone with his tales until the wee hours of the morning."

Charlotte's heart swelled with warmth as she listened, feeling the echoes of laughter and camaraderie reverberating through the room. It seemed as if the walls themselves had absorbed the memories, imbuing the very air with a sense of history and belonging.

"Then there were the two sisters, who arrived here during a terrible storm one winter," Marge went on, her eyes distant as she recalled the memory. "They were so frightened, but our little inn provided them with shelter and comfort. I'll never forget the gratitude in their eyes."

As Marge shared these snippets of the inn's past, Charlotte found herself folding each story into her own heart, tucking them away like cherished keepsakes. The weight of responsibility became not just a burden, but an honor - one she would carry with pride and purpose.

"Thank you for sharing these stories with me," Charlotte said, her voice thick with emotion. "I promise to do my best to continue the inn's legacy, to make it a place where new memories are made and cherished."

Marge looked at her with a warm smile, her eyes glistening with unshed tears. "I know you will, my dear. I have no doubt that The Crown Inn will thrive under your care."

As Marge spoke, Charlotte's eyes darted around the room, taking in the little details that made the inn so unique. She noticed a faint crack on the wooden mantel and wondered if it was simply the result of age or if there was a story behind it. In her heart, she knew that every nook and cranny held a narrative waiting to be discovered.

"Ah, now this," Marge said as she pointed toward a small, stained glass window nestled in an alcove near the ceiling. "This window is a bit temperamental. You'll want to be careful when you open it - sometimes it sticks, and you don't want to break the glass."

Charlotte listened intently as Marge continued dispensing her advice, every word a lesson in caring for the beloved inn. The warmth in Marge's voice conveyed not just knowledge but also a deep affection for the old house.

"Always give the boiler a good kick when it starts making that awful clanging noise," Marge advised with a chuckle. "And remember to trim back the ivy near the gutters. It can be quite persistent."

They paused their packing ritual for a moment, sharing cups of steaming tea and leaning against the now-empty shelves. Their laughter filled the air, intertwining with the fading sunlight that streamed through the windows.

"Did I ever tell you about the time a young couple decided to have their wedding here?" Marge asked, her face lighting up at the memory. "Not the first one I mentioned, but it was such a beautiful ceremony - they exchanged their vows under the old oak tree out back. They come back every year now to celebrate their anniversary."

"Really? That's so lovely," Charlotte said, her heart swelling with joy at the thought of such enduring love finding a home within the inn's walls.

"Indeed," Marge agreed, a wistful smile playing on her lips. "I've seen so many lives touched and changed here. The inn has a way of bringing people together, and I know you'll continue that tradition."

Marge's wisdom and encouragement would be invaluable in the days to come, and she vowed to honor the trust placed in her by ensuring that The Crown Inn remained a symbol of comfort and joy for all who entered its doors.

"I can't believe it's really happening," she murmured, her voice tinged with both awe and trepidation. "It's such an incredible opportunity, but I'm so afraid I won't be able to live up to the legacy you've created here."

Marge placed a reassuring hand on Charlotte's shoulder, her eyes meeting those of her younger counterpart with warmth and conviction. "My dear, I knew from the moment we met that you were destined for great things. You have the passion, the creativity, and the grit needed to make The Crown flourish under your care. Trust in yourself, Charlotte. I do."

The rooms gradually emptied out, leaving behind echoes of laughter, whispered secrets, and tender moments shared within their walls. Each item they packed represented a piece of the inn's rich past, and Charlotte felt a sense of awe and responsibility settle over her like a warm, heavy blanket.

"Almost there," Marge murmured, brushing a strand of hair from her forehead. "You're doing a great job, Charlotte."

"Thanks to you," Charlotte replied, her voice filled with admiration and gratitude. "I'm so grateful for your guidance and friendship, Marge."

"And I'm grateful for the chance to pass this place on to someone who will cherish it as I have," Marge said, her eyes shining with sincerity. "Now, let's finish up. There's still much to do. Even with me taking all these trinkets, this house will still be full of junk for you to deal with!"

"Marge! It's not junk at all. I'm going to love every treasure you leave me. The library alone is like a dream."

The final box was sealed, and the rooms stood mostly bare, their once-crowded corners now echoing with the memories of years gone by. Charlotte took a moment to walk through the inn, her footsteps echoing softly as she marveled at the space that would soon be filled with her own dreams and ambitions.

She paused in the doorway of what used to be Marge's bedroom, her eyes tracing the floral wallpaper. She could almost hear the older woman's laughter still lingering in the air, and it brought a smile to her face.

"Charlotte," Marge called from downstairs, her voice gentle but insistent. "Come here for a moment, please."

Descending the staircase, Charlotte found Marge standing in the foyer, a small velvet box clasped in her hands. Her blue eyes seemed to hold a secret, and Charlotte felt a flutter of anticipation in her chest.

"Before you officially take over The Crown Inn, I have something for you." Marge opened the box, revealing a single brass key nestled within the satin lining. "This is the original key to the inn, handed down through generations. And now, it's yours."

Charlotte reached out, her fingers trembling as they closed around the cool metal. The weight of the key seemed to carry with it the gravity of the responsibility now resting on her shoulders. As she held it, she felt the history of the inn, the laughter and tears shared within its walls, and the love that had been poured into it by countless hands before hers.

"Thank you, Marge," she whispered, her voice thick with emotion. "I promise I will do everything in my power to make you proud and honor the legacy you've built here."

Marge smiled, her eyes glistening with unshed tears. "I know you will, Charlotte. You have a heart as big as this house."

As Charlotte clutched the key to her chest, she felt a mix of excitement and fear stirring within her. The future stretched out before her like an unwritten book, each blank page waiting to be filled with new stories and memories. She knew there would be challenges and setbacks along the way, but with Marge's guidance, she was ready to embrace whatever lay ahead.

With the last box securely fastened, Charlotte and Marge stood in the now-empty foyer of the inn. The echoes of their footsteps on the wooden floor seemed to reverberate through the generations that had passed between these walls. As they looked around at the vacant rooms, a bittersweet silence fell between them.

"Van will be by in the mornin," Marge said, her voice thick. She wrapped Charlotte in one last, tight hug, and then swept away to a waiting car, piloted by none other than Winston, the grandson. As Marge's car pulled away from the inn, Charlotte remained in the doorway, her heart aching. Her hands clenched around the key Marge had entrusted her with, its cool metal serving as a tangible reminder of the responsibility she now carried.

"Here we go," Charlotte whispered to herself, taking a deep breath as she stepped back into the empty inn, ready to begin this new chapter of her life.

She turned on her heels and stepped back inside the inn. Her heart now raced as she walked through the empty rooms, the fading light filtering through the windows casting a warm, nostalgic hue over the spaces she would soon fill with new memories.

She paused in the doorway of the living room. A sense of calm washed over her as she closed her eyes, allowing herself to absorb the energy that surrounded her. Crossing to the mantel of the big fireplace that took up nearly the whole back wall, Charlotte placed the key there. Then, digging in the back pocket of her jeans, she pulled out the old photo of her, Roxanne, and their father, placing one corner in the large, clover-shaped head of the key. Her past and her present, together.

She would hang her painting of The Crown right above this fireplace for all to see. And to remind herself of where it had all began. Charlotte stood there as the sun sank below the horizon, the last of its light disappearing behind the rolling hills. The inn fell into shadow, but Charlotte felt illuminated from within. She knew that with love, determination, and the support of those who believed in her, she could take on any challenge that lay ahead.

She could feel the history of The Crown and all the lives that had passed through its doors, and she knew now she was meant to be a part of that story.

NOW AVAILABLE!

A NEW CHANCE
(Inn by the Sea—Book 2)

In this new romantic comedy series by #1 bestseller Fiona Grace, Charlotte Moore finds herself at a crossroads in life when her husband abruptly divorces her, leaving her with a failed marriage. Desperate for a fresh start, she makes a bold and impulsive decision to invest her last savings in a dilapidated inn on the picturesque seaside coast of the U.K. As Charlotte takes ownership of the inn and begins its restoration, she faces the twin challenges of running a business and navigating her love life—torn between her blossoming romance with a kindred spirit and the unexpected return of her ex-husband.

As she opens the door and breathes life into the historic inn, she might just find her own chance at a new life and a new love...

"Wow, this book takes off & never stops! I couldn't put it down! Highly recommended for those who love a great mystery with twists, turns, romance, and a long lost family member! I am reading the next book right now!"
--Amazon reviewer (regarding *Murder in the Manor*)

"Wish all books were this good a mystery romance and love. Did not want to stop reading this book—loved it."
--Amazon reviewer (regarding *Murder in the Manor*)

A NEW CHANCE is book #2 in a new romance series by #1 bestselling author Fiona Grace, whose books have received over 10,000 five-star reviews and ratings.

Upon her arrival to the seaside coast of England, Charlotte is immediately captivated by the enchanting surroundings and the crumbling historic house perched on the cliffs. With her artistic spirit, she can't resist the allure of the house's faded beauty and the promise of a new canvas for her life, and decides to take up painting again.

As her renovation begins, Charlotte stumbles upon a local man, a rugged fisherman, who at first seems like just another village face— but, beneath the surface, is a man with a vision.

In this heartwarming and inspiring romance series, Charlotte discovers the magic of daily life and the beauty of second chances, rekindling her dreams of purpose and romance in the charming, historic setting of the British coast.

A sweet romance series filled with twists at every turn, INN BY THE SEA will make you laugh and cry as it transports you to a magical place. A page-turner packed with jaw-dropping twists, impossible to put down, it will make you fall in love with romance all over again.

Future books in the series are also available!

"The story line wasn't just a who done it, but had a story about her life and romance, including village life. Very entertaining."
--Amazon reviewer (regarding *Murder in the Manor*)

"It has endearing and sometimes quirky characters, a plot that keeps you reading and the right amount of romance. I can't wait to start book two!"
--Amazon reviewer (regarding *Murder in the Manor*)

"What a great story of murder, romance, new beginnings, love, friend ships and a wonderful cascade of mystery."
--Amazon reviewer (regarding *Murder in the Manor*)

Fiona Grace

Fiona Grace is author of the LACEY DOYLE COZY MYSTERY series, comprising nine books; of the TUSCAN VINEYARD COZY MYSTERY series, comprising seven books; of the DUBIOUS WITCH COZY MYSTERY series, comprising three books; of the BEACHFRONT BAKERY COZY MYSTERY series, comprising six books; of the CATS AND DOGS COZY MYSTERY series, comprising nine books; of the ELIZA MONTAGU COZY MYSTERY series, comprising nine books (and counting); of the ENDLESS HARBOR ROMANTIC COMEDY series, comprising nine books (and counting); of the INN AT DUNE ISLAND ROMANTIC COMEDY series, comprising five books (and counting); of the INN BY THE SEA ROMANTIC COMEDY series, comprising five books (and counting); and of the MAID AND THE MANSION COZY MYSTERY series, comprising five books (and counting).

Fiona would love to hear from you, so please visit www.fionagraceauthor.com to receive free ebooks, hear the latest news, and stay in touch.

A FLAPPER FATALITY (Book #5)
BUMPED BY A DAME (Book #6)
A DOLL'S DEBACLE (Book #7)
A FELLA'S RUIN (Book #8)
A GAL'S OFFING (Book #9)

LACEY DOYLE COZY MYSTERY
MURDER IN THE MANOR (Book#1)
DEATH AND A DOG (Book #2)
CRIME IN THE CAFE (Book #3)
VEXED ON A VISIT (Book #4)
KILLED WITH A KISS (Book #5)
PERISHED BY A PAINTING (Book #6)
SILENCED BY A SPELL (Book #7)
FRAMED BY A FORGERY (Book #8)
CATASTROPHE IN A CLOISTER (Book #9)

TUSCAN VINEYARD COZY MYSTERY
AGED FOR MURDER (Book #1)
AGED FOR DEATH (Book #2)
AGED FOR MAYHEM (Book #3)
AGED FOR SEDUCTION (Book #4)
AGED FOR VENGEANCE (Book #5)
AGED FOR ACRIMONY (Book #6)
AGED FOR MALICE (Book #7)

DUBIOUS WITCH COZY MYSTERY
SKEPTIC IN SALEM: AN EPISODE OF MURDER (Book #1)
SKEPTIC IN SALEM: AN EPISODE OF CRIME (Book #2)
SKEPTIC IN SALEM: AN EPISODE OF DEATH (Book #3)

BEACHFRONT BAKERY COZY MYSTERY
BEACHFRONT BAKERY: A KILLER CUPCAKE (Book #1)
BEACHFRONT BAKERY: A MURDEROUS MACARON (Book #2)
BEACHFRONT BAKERY: A PERILOUS CAKE POP (Book #3)
BEACHFRONT BAKERY: A DEADLY DANISH (Book #4)
BEACHFRONT BAKERY: A TREACHEROUS TART (Book #5)
BEACHFRONT BAKERY: A CALAMITOUS COOKIE (Book #6)

CATS AND DOGS COZY MYSTERY

Made in the USA
Las Vegas, NV
30 January 2024

85116867R00090